THROWAWAY DAUGHTER

THROWAWAY DAUGHTER

Ting-xing Ye

with William Bell

To: Joan,

All the best!

Tingxing Ye
April, 2003

DOUBLEDAY CANADA

Doubleday Canada and colophon are trademarks.

National Library of Canada Cataloguing in Publication

Ye, Ting-xing, 1952–
Throwaway daughter / Ting-xing Ye ; with William Bell.
ISBN 0–385–65952–0
I. Bell, William, 1945–   II. Title.
PS8597.E16T49 2003   C813'.54   C2002–904613–0   PZ7

Cover image: Paul Chesley/Getty Images
Cover design: CS Richardson
Printed and bound in Canada

Published in Canada by Doubleday Canada,
a division of Random House of Canada Limited

Visit Random House of Canada Limited's website: www.randomhouse.ca

TRANS 10 9 8 7 6 5 4 3 2 1

For my daughter, Qi-meng

Who can tell
where the waters carry blossoms
cast upon them?

—Wu Qing-zi, *The Scholars*

Marrying off a daughter is like
throwing away a bucket of water.

—A Chinese saying

The People's
Republic of China

Beijing •

Jiangsu Province
Shanghai •

• Hong Kong

PROLOGUE

❀

No one seemed to understand what it was like to have no real birthday. Even Blackie, our Shih-Tzu, had one, noted on the form given to me when Mom put my name down as his adoptive "parent" when I was five years old. Never mind how that affected my understanding of the word *adoption*. Blackie's registration form even recorded his family history, the whole pedigree.

Lucky me. I had a made-up birthday—December 8, 1980, the day I was found on the steps of the orphanage. I could have been weeks old or a couple of days young; I didn't know and neither did anybody else. I might as well be a lake discovered by an explorer.

My name is Grace Dong-mei Margaret Parker, but don't call me anything but Grace Parker, *without* initials. Grace is my nanna's name, and Margaret is the first name of Grandmamma, my mother's mother. When I came along I ended a silent battle between my two grandmothers that had smouldered ever since my sister was born. Megan was Grandmamma's middle name, but Nanna only won a spot as my sister's middle name, Carole. It became a bigger deal, I guess, after my mom had a hysterectomy.

My name has Chinese in it thanks to my pig-headed parents. I did everything I could to change their minds. I begged, argued, and threw tantrums. All I wanted was to have my Chinese name, Dong-mei, removed. "I promise I'll never, ever ask for anything else," I pleaded. But my pathetic begging failed. So I tried playing dumb and deaf, with my mother especially, refusing to respond when she called me Dong-mei. I made fun of the sound, saying "done-mine" or, once, "dung-may" because I thought it was a dirty word.

My mother applied her teacher's patience and reasoning like sticky ointments. "It's not just a name, Grace; it means much more. Your dad and I promised Mrs. Xia that we would bring you up in touch with your culture and your roots. The name is a good place to start."

"I don't know any Mrs. Whatever," I shouted. "Why do I want their roots? I don't want to be Chinese, and I don't want a Chinese name."

Finally, Mom came up with one of her "reasonable" compromises. Up 'til then, she had called me Dong-mei only at home. If I didn't stop fussing, she said, she'd use my Chinese name outside our house as well. My resistance crumbled.

As if there wasn't enough repeating or reusing names, my confusion deepened when my grade three teacher, Miss McKerrow, taught us a new word, *junior*. She used a boy's name in my class as an example.

"Robert Smith Junior," she said loudly before she wrote the name on the blackboard, "because Rob's father is also called Robert."

Rob, who always needed a haircut and smelled bad, beamed at the attention he was getting. He stood up and told the class that in his family there were three Robs and two Juniors. "My grandfather is the first Robert. My dad and I are Juniors. Whenever my grandfather stays with us there's a mix-up."

That evening I told my mother that I wanted to be a junior, too. I didn't have much idea what the term meant, even after Miss McKerrow's little lesson, but I was pretty sure I was missing out on something, and that it wasn't fair. After the dishes were done Mom sat me down and said that only boys could be Juniors. It was a sort of tradition that boys were named after their fathers or grandfathers. It seemed to me that boys enjoyed a lot more choices than I did.

My parents insisted on feeding me memories of the misery in my life before I came to Canada, which, to me, was no misery at all because I didn't remember it. They told me about my abandonment, my life in an orphanage, their journey to China to adopt me. Little by little they let the details out, as if they were rehearsing a well-directed play, every scene written with extra care and consideration.

But it was as if these tragic events had happened to someone else. I hated my parents' narratives about a stranger, even if the stranger was me. I was sick of seeing the sacred scrap of paper on which there were some marks in faded blue ink. According to my father, it had been hidden

3

between the layers of blankets I was wrapped in when I was found outside the orphanage.

"Dong-mei," my mother pronounced awkwardly, pointing at the second line. "Mr. Wu says it means Winter Plumblossom." Her finger then moved up and she spoke again. "Chun-mei, Spring Plum-blossom, is the name of your birth mother. Mrs. Xia from the orphanage told us that."

Since I was born in the winter, probably at the time when winter plum trees were in flower, Chun-mei must have been born in the spring. In China it was traditional to name girls after flowers, Mom went on, adding that the note must have been written and tucked into my blanket by my birth mother. "Obviously the names are very important to her or she wouldn't have taken such a risk."

"It's a stupid name," I snapped. "I don't want to be named after some dumb flower. Why didn't this Chun-mei keep the baby and throw away the note?"

As far as I was concerned, the note as well as my Chinese roots could wither in hell.

PART ONE

Milford, Ontario

GRACE

❀

As well as being a "tearless girl," according to what Mom and Dad had been told when they took delivery of me like a FedEx package, I was born deaf. I did not react to sound or show emotion. It was my sister who claimed credit for uncovering the truth.

Megan's story, which changes a bit every time she tells it, is this: On my first night in my new home, Megan insisted that Mom bring me to her room and put me down on her bed for a while. She wanted to get an early start on being Big Sister. Mom turned her back for a moment to pick up some clothes my new sister had left lying on the bathroom floor. She heard a *pop!* followed by a wail.

"I didn't mean it!" Megan shouted.

My mother rushed from the bathroom and the two of them stood at the side of the bed staring down at me. I lay on my back, holding a potato chip in each hand, giggling and making other baby noises. When Megan had popped open the bag of chips my eyes had bugged out and I let out a cry. She had given me the chips to shut me up.

My supposed birth defect had been a mistake.

For years, especially when my family invited Mr. Wu over, I wished that I *had* been born deaf.

I was seven when I met Frank Wu for the first time. He had been introduced to Mom through another teacher in her school. Mom and Dad became friends with him, talking to him often on the phone. His name was frequently brought up at our house. Frank said this, Frank suggested that—as if he were some kind of encyclopedia on my "culture and heritage." I already disliked him.

One Sunday morning before March break, the four of us drove to the city and met Mr. Wu in front of a Chinese restaurant downtown. He shook hands with my parents and Megan, but when he got to me he patted me on the top of my head, smiling and letting out a goofy laugh, *shee-shee-shee.*

"I am so glad to see you, Glace," he said, squatting so he could talk to me at eye level, his face inches from mine. I didn't appreciate being patted like a dog, or the way he pronounced my name. He smelled like mothballs, and dandruff sprinkled the shoulders of his shabby coat.

"It's Gr—" I began but shut up when I saw the stern look my mother was giving me. "Nice to meet you, too," I mumbled, wondering if he called himself "Flank."

The New and Bright Restaurant should have been called Crammed and Smelly. As we followed Mr. Wu in single file though the crowded, noisy waiting room, Megan pointed to a gigantic fish tank. She whispered that all the sad-looking fish, half-dead lobsters, and spidery crabs were going to end up, cooked, on people's plates.

"Don't be gross!" I hissed.

"If you don't believe me, ask Mr. Wu, *Glace*."

When we were seated at one of the many large round tables, surrounded by strange smells and hundreds of people talking at once, I looked about. The red walls were covered with paintings of pine trees and cranes, tigers and pandas, mountains and waterfalls. At one end, a dragon hung opposite some kind of bird, both in bright gold. Waitresses walked up and down the aisles, pushing carts of food from table to table, reflected in the mirrors that covered the entire left wall, making the room look ten times bigger than it was. I had never been to a place where people who looked like me made up the majority—a sea of Asian faces, brown eyes, black hair. At most of the tables, everyone in the family had the same complexion and colouring. Just then I realized I had never been as close to a Chinese person as I was to Mr. Wu at that moment.

"They fooled me, too," he said, smiling at me. "The mirrors, the first time I came here."

"Oh?" I answered, uninterested in anything he had to say. Then I remembered my mother's repeated commands to be polite to Flank. "It's neat," I quickly added.

Megan was doing her big sister act, on her best behaviour, trying to act like one of the adults and butting in on their conversation. Mr. Wu and my parents were having a good time, yakking away as small plates of food were put on the table—weird-looking stuff that I'd never seen before in my life. Even my dad looked panicky when a plate of chicken feet appeared. They looked gross but I had to admit they smelled tasty. I picked at my food, nibbled at some steamed rice mixed with soy sauce. I already planned to ask if we could stop at a fast-food joint on the way home for a bag of fries. Maybe a burger, too, depending on my mood.

Since I didn't have much else to do, I listened in on the conversation. I learned that Mr. Wu had been born in China and that he had come to Canada five years after I had. His family was still back in China. China is not a good place to live, he told my parents. There is no freedom, and your life is not your own. Now he lived above a grocery store near the restaurant.

I wondered why he would have given up a teaching job in China to bus tables and wash dishes in a restaurant at night and stock shelves in a grocery store on the weekends. Occasionally he made some extra money by giving private Chinese lessons. He looked poor, yet he didn't look unhappy.

I nibbled some more rice and looked around. I noticed the family gatherings all around me included at least three generations—babies, teenagers, parents, grandparents whose hair had gone white, enough adults to mean uncles and aunts, enough kids to mean cousins. It struck me for the first time in my life that I had a whole bunch of relatives in China. And did they know they had a relative in Canada named Grace?

JANE

❀

(1981)

When I asked Megan, who was turning seven in a few weeks, what she would like for her birthday, she piped up, "A sister!" Her words struck my heart like stones.

Kevin and I were from small families. We knew when we got married that we wanted a big family, but it didn't turn out that way.

There had been a time when I began every day wishing evening would come quickly so I could lose myself in sleep. I spent the day in my housecoat and slippers. I didn't bathe or comb my hair. Sometimes, when he came home from the office at noon to check on me, Kevin found me where he had left me, sitting on the couch, staring at nothing.

I didn't feel sorry for myself; I didn't feel anything. I changed my dressings with the disinterest of a cop writing a traffic ticket. Sometimes I wandered from room to room in the empty house, aimlessly picking up toys, knick-knacks, books, magazines, turning them over in my hands and setting them down again. I yearned to be interested in things.

Kevin phoned from work every hour or so. I let the machine pick up. After the first sympathy call from the school where I taught, I wanted no more. I couldn't bear the honeyed tone of voice, the soft concern, the kindness that grated like broken glass. The solicitations of Kevin's and my parents set my teeth on edge. When they came over I screamed silently for them to go away, to ease my burning nerves. Megan, bewildered by the woman her mother had become, avoided me. Kevin understood. He left me alone, but seemed to know where I was every second.

When the anger came, seeping into me the way spilled blood soaks a paper towel, I welcomed it. For a time, rage was my friend. Unable to rail against god or fate, I cursed the doctors. The operation left me empty and barren as sand. The thought of the hospital churned my fury. On one floor people in white smocks struggled to bring another day's life to a premature infant in an incubator, while on the floor below others casually performed abortion after abortion. The absurdity was cosmic. I was somewhere in the middle. My baby lost through miscarriage, what they clinically called my reproductive system damaged beyond hope. And removed, leaving me empty and bitter for a long time.

Megan must have overheard conversations between Kevin and me, and the phone calls with adoption agencies. A few wouldn't even give us appointments after they learned that we already had a girl of our own. Those who had finally agreed to interview us marked us down on their long waiting lists with little hope.

We eventually stopped talking about adopting altogether. Until Megan brought it up again.

It was a typical fall day. The sky was a vast sea of blue, embellishing a forest of coloured leaves. I was in the staff room at lunchtime, waiting for my lunch to heat up in the microwave, when I noticed a newspaper clipping pinned to the bulletin board. It was a brief report on China's family-planning law. As a grade four teacher, most of my reading was confined to student projects on insects and reptiles, or spelling tests and arithmetic quizzes. When I did get a chance to branch out, I settled down with something refreshingly literary, so I knew very little in detail about China. But I had a husband addicted to his three newspapers a day and a father who was a retired head librarian, so I had picked up a bit of information. China was changing, opening up more and more to trade and tourism. By the end of the week, after talking to both Kevin and Dad, I had a good grasp of China's attempts at population control. And the more I learned, the deeper I was drawn into what I came to call China's baby policy, which allowed only one child per family and strictly punished parents who broke the rule. They were subject to fines, demotions, and ejection from the Communist Party, and a cruel second-class citizenship awaited the forbidden second child. But one thing we discovered with delight: people outside China were allowed to adopt Chinese babies.

I called the Children's Aid Society in Toronto. An agent advised me to get in touch with the federal government's International Adoption Desk in Ottawa. They in turn told me to write to a certain private adoption agency in Vancouver, which had in the past couple of years brought back overseas children to homes in Canada; a few of them were from China. The woman who answered the phone informed me that the agency had no problem accepting applicants who already had kids. But I would have to take an older child, she told me, or one with a disability or questionable health. Or a girl, if the child is Chinese, I said to myself.

After months of phone calls and tons of paperwork, a letter arrived with a photo of a little girl named Dong-mei. The poor thing looked too small for a six-month-old. Along with the picture came instructions to apply for a Chinese visa, and more documents and forms to be filled in by our family doctor, employers, and banks. Megan was delighted by all the official forms, and we watched her go through them page by page as we looked at each other across the kitchen table. Suddenly it had all become real.

The colour photo showed me nothing about the child who, if all the bureaucrats could be satisfied, was going to be our daughter. How could a baby's face be so grave and blank?

On Tuesday afternoon when I got home from school, there were three phone messages from a reporter at *The Milford Daily*, asking us to return his call as soon as possible.

"Mrs. Parker, this is a fascinating story," he pressed me when I called back. "A Red Chinese baby is coming to Milford and—"

"Mr. Jenkins, I understand that you have a job to do. But at the moment I have nothing to say."

A few days later, on the front page of the paper, was the headline "Milford's First Chinese Citizen." I read the article, trembling with anger. At least he hadn't brought politics in; there was no mention of "red."

But I had more on my mind than a newspaper story. In a letter we received a day earlier, via the adoption agency, we learned for the first time that Dong-mei had been born deaf. That surely explained her sad face in the photo. But why had we not been told until two weeks before we headed across the Pacific to get her? I went through every single letter sent to us and failed to find even a hint about the child's disability. A phone call to Vancouver didn't help much. All I got was an earful of apologies from Ms. Chow, who promised to look into the matter as soon as she could. I wasn't interested in who was responsible or where to lay the blame. It was no one's fault if Dong-mei was deaf. What would matter to me, and to Kevin and Megan, was whether or not her disability would change our decision.

Ms. Chow called me back three days later. She related that Chinese government policy dictated that if the adoptee was a second child as in our case, the adopting family must accept an "imperfect" baby. The rule also applied within China but in reverse. Only couples whose first child is deformed are allowed a second. Chow added that if I changed my mind about adopting Dong-mei I should let her know as soon as possible.

I'd like to say that Kevin and I weren't bothered by this new development. But we both tossed and turned in the darkness. Say what you will, a disabled child brings added responsibility, strain on the family, expense, and demands on emotional energy. I knew that from being a teacher for years. And if Dong-mei's hearing impairment had been kept from us, what other problems might the Chinese bureaucrats have overlooked—or hidden?

We got up in the morning, carried on our normal routine. My mind, though, was a stormy sea, and as the day wore on I became more agitated.

"Would we have given up Megan if she was born deaf or mute?" I asked Kevin as soon as he stepped into the house that evening.

Kevin looked at me with the same sense of determination that had attracted me on our first date. "Let's do it, Jane."

I picked up the phone. For the first time since our contact with the adoption agency I was thankful that Vancouver was three hours behind. "Nothing has changed," I told Ms. Chow. "We are going to China as scheduled."

The Nanjing Hotel was a rather forbidding Russian-style pile of stone set in a garden in the northeast part of the city of Nanjing. The trees and hedges surrounding the building drooped in the heat.

"Ten days?" the young woman at the front desk said incredulously.

There followed rapid dialogue, frowning, and head-shaking between the clerk and Ms. Cai, the woman from the Nanjing Foreign Affairs Office who had met us at the airport and would be our interpreter and liaison with the orphanage. Kevin and I exchanged glances.

"Ten?" the clerk asked again, this time in English, holding up both hands with her fingers splayed. "Here? Nanjing?"

While Kevin filled out the registration form, I asked Ms. Cai, "Is everything all right? The hotel isn't full, is it?"

This brought a laugh from the interpreter. Cai was a small woman in her mid-forties, garbed in a white blouse and black trousers. "Oh, no, Mrs. Parker." She pronounced it Pokka. "Everything just fine. No problem at all. The young comrade is curious about your long staying. In summer, Nanjing is known as one of China's 'three furnaces,' so tourists usually try to avoid to come here. Or to have short visit at least."

I looked at the clerk. "Please tell the young lady that where we come from it is winter six months of the year. We don't mind a bit of hot weather."

After Cai translated, the young woman smiled behind her hand. "Wer-come," she said.

Although our room had an air conditioner that wheezed away at the window, I would be stretching things if I claimed it was cool. It was frustrating, sitting in our room, bathed in our own sweat, waiting to see Dong-mei. The closer we came to seeing her, the more anxious we became that something might go wrong.

Ms. Cai was all right, doing what she was supposed to do—acting as a go-between and tour guide—with grace and politeness. The pumpkin-faced woman tried her best to help us occupy our time. Upon meeting us, she had handed me a typed itinerary of sights to see. But after a tedious trip to the Sun Yat-sen tomb the next morning, I pitched the itinerary directly into the garbage.

While we were having lunch in the hotel restaurant, Ms. Cai came to inform us that our request to visit the orphanage in

Yangzhou had been turned down. Yangzhou, about two and a half hours by bus from Nanjing, sits where the Grand Canal meets the Yangtze River.

Kevin and I were learning that asking "Why?" didn't often produce acceptable answers. Or answers that made sense.

"There are no bus tickets," Ms. Cai said to us.

Kevin looked at me, then asked Ms. Cai, "How can there be no tickets? It's a public transit system, isn't it? It operates daily, doesn't it?"

"We'll take a taxi tomorrow," I cut in. "If we leave in the morning, we'll be there before noon. Plenty of time to look around, then return."

"Not possible," Ms. Cai said firmly. "The orphanage is not *kai-fang-dan-wei*. It is not open to foreign visitors."

"Wouldn't it have been easier to tell us that earlier on in the conversation?" Kevin muttered.

"But we don't care about the facilities," I protested. "We just want to see the place where Dong-mei has lived, maybe take a few pictures to show her when she's older. It's important to us that Dong-mei keeps a link to her heritage, her roots."

Cai sounded puzzled. "But why you want her to know such negative details? The dark part of her life? Her mother deserted her. When they found her, she was half frozen, didn't have strength to eat or cry. The workers in the orphanage called her Tearless Girl. Then later they realized her hearing defect. It's sad story. Better she not know. She a lucky girl, just tell her that."

Days passed. The streets sweltered. A thunderstorm howled across the city. Kevin and I tried to while away the time reading, going for walks in the relative cool of evening, occasionally succumbing to Cai's urgings to accompany her to a temple or other historic site. Gnawed by doubt, we reminded ourselves that everything had gone well—though slowly—so far, and we had nothing to fear. We were also aware that as Canadians we were favoured by China to adopt their children. We knew that the memory of Norman Bethune was still strong, and that he was still regarded as a hero and great friend of the Chinese people. Canada's being one of the first Western nations to recognize Mao Ze-dong's government also helped, we thought.

"If this is how they treat people they favour," Kevin joked, "I hate to think how it would be if we were not favoured."

The sixth morning began as the others had. The heat came with the light, and by breakfast time the cicadas were thrumming in the gardens. We had just finished our meal and returned to our room when there was a knock on the door. It was Ms. Cai, her chubby face split by a triumphant grin that made my heart soar. Standing on one side of her was an older man whose white shirt was buttoned to his chin; on the other, a middle-aged woman similarly dressed, with short straight hair as rigid as her posture. In her arms was a bundle of blankets.

"Kevin!" I called out, forgetting to invite the party in.

Kevin rushed to the door. "Come in, please," he urged.

The woman said something.

"We may have overdressed Dong-mei," Cai translated. "We heard that the hotel is air-conditioned and didn't want her to catch a chill."

I let out a nervous laugh at the word *chill*.

After we had persuaded our visitors to sit, Cai began to speak formally. "Allow me to introduce Mr. Liu, director of Social and Welfare Institute of Jiangsu Province. Mrs. Xia is with Yangzhou Orphanage, which is under the leadership of the institute. It was Mrs. Xia who found Dong-mei outside the orphanage over seven months ago."

While Cai talked, I made tea and set the cups on the tables beside our guests, who ignored them. Mr. Liu cleared his throat and began to talk in a surprisingly powerful voice.

"Mr. and Mrs. Parker. Your patience is appreciated by our government, and your donation to the orphanage is very generous. Perhaps all the paperwork required for Dong-mei's adoption is in order. So, if you would sign this document, you may take Dong-mei to Canada." The document, we were informed, was actually a receipt, dated and stamped, acknowledging that we had received a female child from the institution.

While the translation pattered on, Kevin and I couldn't tear our eyes from the motionless bundle in Xia's arms. We signed where Cai indicated and returned the papers to Mr. Liu. Liu then stood, followed by Xia and Cai.

"Now I'm sure you are eager to see your daughter," he said kindly. "If you have no more questions, we will go."

He gestured to Xia to hand over the baby, whose face we had yet to see. I took her and immediately pulled the outer blankets away to reveal the same tiny, serious face that I had seen in the photo. "Thank you, thank you," was all I could say.

Xia rattled off a few sentences and Cai translated.

"Mrs. Xia tells that you should feed the baby soy milk, maybe with a little sugar. Also once a day you may give a bit fruit or rice made into mush."

"Yes," I said, gazing down into the tiny face of my daughter, "I brought soy milk with me."

"Please convey our thanks to the Chinese government and the officials at Yangzhou Orphanage," Kevin intoned, as formally as he could manage. "There is one request I would like to make. My wife and I wonder if there is any information on Dong-mei's background. We would like to know as much as we can in case Dong-mei asks us when she is older."

There was a moment of silence. Cai looked a little displeased after she had finished the translation. Liu shook his head. "*Mei-you*—nothing," was all he said.

Cai elaborated. "Whoever left Dong-mei did it secretly. If seen, the person would have been punished and the baby returned."

Xia kept silent, looking at the floor. After more formal thank-yous and farewells, the three Chinese left us with our new daughter.

As soon as the door was closed I lay Dong-mei on the bed and began to loosen the tightly wrapped blankets.

"Three layers! It's a wonder the poor little mite didn't roast. Look, Kevin, she's so small!"

But she was bright-eyed and she kicked and punched, blowing bubbles as I removed her soggy cotton diaper and put on one of the disposable ones we had brought with us. It was far too large, and, as if aware of how pathetic she looked in it, Dong-mei began to cry.

I picked her up, swaddled in a light cotton blanket, and began to pace the room to quiet her. No luck. I sat down and bounced her on my knees. Dong-mei wailed even louder, and I was grateful that the hotel was almost empty. Kevin took her from me and sang to her, with no effect.

It was a long night. We took turns walking and rocking our little girl, who after a few hours quieted down—provided she was in motion. As soon as she was placed on the bed, her eyes would snap open and the cries would come again. An hour or so before dawn, Dong-mei drifted off to sleep, and I lay her between us on the bed. In seconds, the three of us were asleep.

I was awakened by a quiet knock at the door. "What's that?" I exclaimed.

I looked at my watch when the knock was repeated, low but insistent. Six am. Still dressed from the night before, I rolled carefully off the bed, picked Dong-mei up, and opened the door.

Mrs. Xia pushed past me into the room and closed the door behind her.

"Oh, no," I moaned. "Kevin, there must be something wrong! Is there a problem?" I asked Xia. She gave me a bewildered look. I remembered she had no English. I asked, "Alone?" She frowned at me. I held up one finger. "Alone?" She seemed to catch on, because she nodded and, to my relief, smiled.

"Um, *you-wen-ti-ma?*" Kevin tried haltingly. "Is there trouble?"

Xia shook her head. "*Bu, bu, bu,*" she said. She made sure

the door was locked, then took a small piece of paper from her pocket and handed it to me.

I said to Kevin, "There's writing on it. In Chinese."

The writing was in blue ink, just four handwritten characters. I wondered why Xia hadn't given it to us the day before so that Ms. Cai could translate it for us. Then it struck me that she had brought it today, alone, at dawn, because it was secret.

Xia pointed to the first line on the paper. "Chun-mei. Mama," she said. Then, pointing to the second, "Dong-mei."

"Is she trying to say that Chun-mei is Dong-mei's mother?" Kevin said to me.

"But they told us yesterday her mother was unknown."

This time I pointed to the first line of writing. "Dong-mei Mama?" I asked Mrs. Xia.

Her face brightened. "*Dui, dui, dui.*" She smiled, touching my finger. "Chun-mei." She then moved my finger to the last two characters. "Dong-mei." She patted the baby's head.

The similarity of names struck me, though I didn't know what they meant. "I understand," I said uselessly.

"I bet the note was left with the baby," Kevin said. "The mother must have wanted the names to be known."

Dong-mei chose that moment to wail as if I had pinched her. Xia took a close look underneath her blanket and noticed the disposable diaper with the big pink flower on the bottom. She *tsk*ed and shook her head and held out her arms. Reluctantly, I handed Dong-mei to her.

Xia put Dong-mei down on the bed and stripped off the diaper. She searched the room with her eyes and pounced on the green canvas bag she had left with us the day before.

From it she removed a worn but clean cotton diaper and, mumbling to herself, pinned it on the baby. Dong-mei fell silent.

Xia pointed to the disposable diaper. "*Bu, bu, bu,*" she said, shaking her head.

She passed Dong-mei to me, then shook hands with Kevin and me.

"I wish I could talk to you—and thank you," I told her.

Xia unlocked the door, opened it, and looked up and down the hall before stepping out. "*Zai-jian,*" she said, and walked briskly to the stairway.

GRACE

❀

One of the many rules of the Parker family is that dinner must never be interrupted by serious conversation. Arguments are strictly forbidden. Polite chit-chat of the "How was your day, dear?" variety is all that's allowed. The sharp bickering that sometimes goes on between Megan and me shuts down as soon as we enter the dining room. Only after the plates have been cleared can any weighty discussion happen.

One autumn day when I was in elementary school I made my way home under a cloud of doom, dragging my feet and seizing any opportunity—walking with my arms held out for balance along the curb, side-stepping cracks in the sidewalk, kicking bunches of soggy leaves along the gutter—to slow me down. Dad's car was in the driveway. When I pushed open the front door I yelled "I'm home!" and ran upstairs to my room.

Dinner was torture. My teacher had told me that she had called Mother at lunchtime. I knew my parents were aware of what I had done—or, more exactly, not done. I knew they wouldn't mention my crime until after dinner, and their calm, purposeful eating infuriated me. Megan's cheerful ignorance of the issue heightened the suspense and her prattling twisted my nerves.

I fiddled with my pork chop, pushed mashed potatoes around on my plate, rolled peas back and forth. My mother pretended not to notice. Dad chomped away noisily, setting my teeth on edge. Mom ate with her usual delicacy, nodding and making encouraging noises as Megan nibbled at her salad and rattled on about the Drama Club elections. She was running for president. She'd win, too. Miss Perfect.

"Can I be excused?" Megan finally asked, throwing down her napkin and pushing back her chair.

"Not yet, dear," Mom replied. "We have something to discuss first."

Megan shot a glance at me, then at Dad. I could see the wheels turning. She was wondering if our parents had found her out, prepared for the possibility that I had broken my promise and told about her sneaking off to Matt's party the previous Friday night. She had told Mom and Dad that she'd be spending the night at her friend Patti's—which was, as with all Megan's subterfuges, partly true. Patti had gone to the party, too. I sat quietly, watching Megan suffer as she decided on the exact proportion of truth and falsehood, composing her lie, grateful for the diversion, even if it would not last.

"Dong-mei, dear," Mother said calmly in her Teacher Voice. "Mrs. Crossly called me today. Would you like to tell us why?"

"Didn't she tell you?"

The corners of her mouth tightened a little. "Your dad and I would like you to explain."

Megan planted her elbows on the table, rested her chin on her hands, looked straight at me, and smiled.

"Well?" Dad said half-heartedly.

"I didn't hand in my project," I confessed.

"Why not?" Mom asked.

"I didn't have one to hand in."

"Because?"

"Because I didn't do it."

Mother let out a sigh. "Dong-mei, stop being obtuse and explain yourself."

Two weeks before, Crossly had announced what she proudly called a special history project. We would have a great deal of leeway, she said, and there would be lots of opportunity to be as creative as we wished. I had assumed *history* meant history, and that *leeway* signified choice.

Mrs. Crossly handed out the assignment the next morning. "It's your *personal* history!" she crowed, as if announcing the winner of a lottery. "And, above all things, exactness and accuracy will be rewarded. All information *must* be correct."

The instructions, detailed and numerous, were printed on pink paper—"So you won't lose them," she had told us. There were lots of blanks to fill in to get us started. My pink sheet remained somewhere in the dust and grime of my desk at school.

One look at it had been enough to awaken the procrastination I was so good at. NAME marked the first blank line. DATE OF BIRTH, the second. CITY OF BIRTH, the third. I dutifully printed Grace Parker at the beginning, then put down my pencil. The fear of being mocked or thought stupid paralyzed me.

I didn't know my date of birth. Yangzhou was the city where the orphanage was situated, but my actual place of birth was as big a mystery as the date. My parents had always held my birthday party on the anniversary of my arrival in Canada, but Mom had carefully explained to me that this was a symbolic date. Mrs. Crossly had stressed, repeatedly, that the details in our personal history project must be "absolutely exact. The evidence is no good if it's not accurate." And I took her literally, certain I'd be found out and criticized if I faked the information.

Below the empty blanks on the pink sheet was a paragraph of instructions that emphasized the need to interview family members, especially grandparents and other relatives, as well as our parents. More blanks had been provided to list the names of those questioned. But who could I interview? I felt as if the whole project had been designed to snare me.

Taking the problem to my parents was not an option. They didn't know anything more than I did. So I sat in class, writing nothing, as kids around me scribbled industriously, putting Milford or Edmonton or Toronto in the third blank.

"I couldn't do it," I said helplessly when Mother once more demanded an explanation. "I couldn't fill in the spaces."

Megan began to remove our plates and load the dishwasher.

"I think I get it," Dad said after a moment. "You didn't know the answers to the questions."

I nodded, staring down at the table, twisting my fingers in my lap.

"What were the questions?" Mom asked.

My eyes stung with tears. "Birthday. Where I was born—that kind of stuff."

"But," Mom began, "why didn't you—?"

"Because all that stuff you told me isn't *real!* And Mrs. Crossly would find out! She'd get me in trouble for putting down lies."

"Why didn't you just make something up?" Megan suggested from the doorway. "Crossly wouldn't know the diff. Or care. It's just a project."

"Megan, that's not very helpful," Mom said.

"Neither is your approach to the whole thing," Dad put in. It was unusual for him to say anything critical to Mother, especially in front of Megan and me. "As far as we're all concerned, Dong-mei was born on August 13, 1981, and that's that. And she was born in Yangzhou. What's the use of telling a child her birthday is only symbolic, for heaven's sake? I told you it would only confuse things. Now look what's happened."

"Well." Mother smoothed her napkin. "Be that as it may, there's still a project that has to be completed."

"I think I should call Crossly and tell her to give Grace a substitute assignment. Or maybe you should call. I'm liable to remind her how insensitive she was to ask Grace to do that project to begin with."

"I'll phone her tomorrow," Mom said. "We'll work it out."

They left the table thinking they had solved something.

PART TWO

❀

Liuhe Village, Jiangsu Province

OLD REVOLUTIONARY CHEN

(1980)

I am called Chen "Big Power." Oh, yes, that's my name—Chen Da-li. When I was young I was one of the tallest and strongest men in our village. I could pull a heavy wooden plow through the tired earth like an ox. And I was often asked to do so because there were not enough oxen to go around in those days. And for us farmers, time is everything. My being an ox earned me double work-points, more than any other farmer in the village.

Behind my back, by then less powerful but just as broad, I was nicknamed Old Revolutionary Chen long before my retirement. I would like to say there was no derision in the label.

Personally, I prefer to be called Secretary Chen. It sounds more respectful, and it reflects the damn truth. I became Party Secretary of my village after years of hard work and loyalty to the Communist Party, responsible for thirty-four households. Fifteen years later, I was promoted to brigade level, overseeing seven villages for nearly a decade. Then came retirement, which was not my decision. By then our great leader, Chairman Mao, was gone, and already the earth was trembling with change.

I could never raise myself to commune level, the highest position in the region, because I couldn't read and write like most of the people there. But I knew by heart Chairman Mao's story "Old Man Yu Moves the Mountain," and that was good enough for me. It was our nation's most sacred tale while the Great Helmsman, Mao Ze-dong, was alive. I personally distributed the little red book in which the story was printed, one for each member of every household. I also arranged to have it read daily through the loudspeakers mounted on hydro poles around the village. In those years, I would go nowhere without a copy of the book in my pocket, even though I couldn't read it. I was as thirsty for Chairman Mao's great wisdom as a drunken sailor is for rice wine.

A long time ago, the story begins, Old Man Yu owned three *mu* of land. But between his wattle house and his fields stood two mountains. Yu and his family wasted hours each day, precious tilling time, going to and fro around the mountains. One day, Old Man Yu decided to move the obstacles. But all he had was a hoe, a couple of bamboo baskets, and a shoulder pole. His neighbours laughed at him, saying his ambition was utter foolishness, a waste of time.

Yu shook his head. "It looks impossible," he agreed. "But when I die, my son will continue the work, and when he passes away, his son will take up the task, and so on. And some day, those mountains will be gone."

When the god of heaven got wind of Old Man Yu's determination, he was so deeply moved that he sent down two of his generals, and they carried the mountain away on their backs. My eyes well up with tears when I think of Chairman Mao. He has been dead more than three years, but not for the first time I wonder if the Great Helmsman would have written this story if he reminded himself that not every man has a line of male descendants, like Old Man Yu did, to carry on his work.

I was never emotional when I was young. In those years I believed that there was no room inside my body to store tears. When, at sixteen, I watched my whole family swallowed by the muddy Yellow River, I didn't cry. Nor did I shed a single drop while I was imprisoned in the "cow shed," ridiculed by the Red Guards during the years of wind and fire—the Cultural Revolution. But when I heard about the death of Chairman Mao, I cried like a baby. I cried sitting down, cried when I was walking. I cried myself awake, then cried some more until I fell asleep again. For days, according to my wife, I couldn't eat, couldn't work, but most of all I couldn't keep my eyes dry. My heart ached as I thought about the good things Chairman Mao had done for me, for my family, for the entire country, especially us peasants. The songs praised him as the sun in the east, the brightest star in the dark sky. Every word was the truth. I felt grateful to my parents because they had given me life to begin with. But it was Chairman Mao who had made it worth living. How could I not feel sad and totally lost upon his death?

My son, whom I had named Zhong—Loyal, showing my devotion to the Chairman and the Communist Party—

said to me one day that it was only natural that my sorrow doubled, even tripled over the death of Chairman Mao because I had never really grieved the drowning of my own parents. That's how young people speak nowadays, some flashing their schooling and talking in circles, some showing off their wealth, some just being plain disrespectful. Like many people his age, Loyal grew up in a honey jar, with no idea what sorrow means. His generation can't even imagine what life was like before Chairman Mao liberated the nation and redistributed the land among the peasants. I would never put my parents on the same level as Chairman Mao. Not when he was alive, nor after his death. With him gone, I didn't feel too terrible about my retirement.

I am not so sure about the sudden, sweeping changes taking place around me. But I am fully aware that I'm getting older. Two months ago, my oldest granddaughter, the first child of my eldest girl, gave birth to a baby boy. Weeks later, at the Lunar New Year, Loyal was married. With my first great-grandson in my arms and a new daughter-in-law added to my family, I came to realize that we all have to stop somewhere so that the young can make a beginning.

The way things have turned out in the past couple of years, I'm glad that I am Party Secretary no more. I would never have dreamed three short years of so-called reform could so quickly overturn thirty years of Chairman Mao's glory. Nor could I imagine his godlike revolutionary greatness being dismissed from our lives at such speed. His little red book has became a relic, a collector's item. With no instructions to follow, I feel like a fish out of water each time I think about my latest challenges.

My daughter-in-law is pregnant. I was beside myself with joy, and relief, when I was told the news. But after I calmed down, I was overcome by the worries I had harboured ever since Loyal's wedding. I had to put on a happy, trouble-free face in front of those who came to offer their congratulations. I smiled, laughed a bit, then smiled some more until my cheeks were stiff. I assured everyone that the gender of the baby was of no consequence. And that was the toughest thing for me to do, much harder than moving a mountain.

I didn't fret like that when I was a father, six times altogether. I was disappointed each time my wife gave birth to a girl child, but not concerned. I kept in mind an old saying my wife loves to recite, that as long as there are green mountains, we have no need to worry about firewood. Eventually my patience was rewarded. Loyal, my sixth child and first son, was born in the fall of 1955, shortly after I turned forty. I was at an age when many men in our region were already grandfathers. One fellow villager said to me that no amount of gold could match my good luck. I criticized his feudal attitude, but in my heart I agreed.

Holding baby Loyal in my arms, I contained myself, showing very little emotion. Although I was a new Communist Party member, I had been long aware of the government propaganda that favouring boys over girls was feudal rubbish. It had taken me many years of backbreaking work and positive attitude to be accepted by the Party, but only days to learn what I should say and not say in public. What I couldn't admit openly was that we farmers needed boys: not only were they the ones to carry on our family names but their muscles and power were essential to keep our stomachs filled. Everywhere I turned my eyes, able-bodied men were called for. Even Chairman Mao agreed, as he showed in the tale he loved to repeat. The Chairman didn't mention one word about girls—Old Man Yu's daughters and granddaughters. Living in the countryside is like moving a mountain; we have to have boys.

I hold nothing against girls; I have five of them. But they are just not as useful and capable as boys. It's particularly so in our region where nature contributes only thirty percent to our survival. Intense labour makes up the rest, so boys are regarded as feeding hands, and girls, as mouths. Some people in the village openly say that raising girls is a money-losing proposition. After years of feeding and clothing them, they leave home, get married, look after people other than their parents, and bear children who carry their husband's name.

Among my five daughters, three are married; one lives nearby and two far away. They all have children, but I seldom see them. That, too, is reality. As soon as the pregnancy of my daughter-in-law was confirmed, the memories I had tried so hard to keep out of my mind returned, like water rushing past a broken dam. My number four and five girls didn't live long enough to see their wedding day. They died very young, during the "years of difficulties" as the Party puts it, or the famine years as Loyal calls them more bluntly, which is typical of him. For a long time I have tried to shut out the memory of my lost girls. Each time their deaths surface in my mind, making me see them wasted to skin and bone, I close my eyes tight as if to squeeze the images out.

Or I try to think of something else. Anything. Sometimes it works, but not always. Recently I find myself getting weaker because I've thought about them so much, and sadness and guilt are the aftermath. I'm glad that years ago Loyal stopped asking me how he, being the youngest among his siblings, had survived, while his two older sisters starved to death. It was not that I didn't want to reply to him; I just didn't know the answer. My wife is fond of saying that not everything in the world has an explanation. I don't agree with her but I don't argue.

The key point of the whole issue is that Loyal and his wife won't get a second chance to have a son if the child is a girl. A family-planning policy that allows only one child to each married couple was laid down by the government, and two years ago the policy was made a strictly enforced law, bearing severe consequences for anyone who doesn't obey. Since then, bad news keeps blowing in my direction. So-and-so was stripped of Party membership for violating the law; such-and-such family lost their precious vegetable plot for breaking the rule. And each lawbreaker is no stranger to me, for I used to be their leader. I would be the one to mete out the punishment if I were still in office.

I'm in a unique situation, being the only Chen among the Liu clan. Every household in our village has Liu as the surname, after the river that runs through the east end. At the age of sixteen, skinny as a rope, I left my native village after my family perished in the flood, and begged my way from Shandong Peninsula to the north shore of the Yangtze River, where a family adopted me and renamed me Liu. I changed it back to Chen soon after I started my own family.

I am the only survivor in my original family, the only root of Chen. I can't bear to see my family tree cease growing.

Last night I had the worst nightmare of my entire life. In the dream, the Yellow River had burst through its banks again and flooded our fields and village. I was tied down on a plank door. While one surge of waves dragged me into the current, the next surfed me up. I struggled as hard as I could, trying to locate my family in the dark, but the raging flood pushed me farther away from them. I was clearly aware that if I lay still, remained on the board, let the waves take me, I might live. But live alone. I was so torn apart in making a decision that my head hurt even after I woke up. My body ached too. I haven't had this kind of nightmare for years. The only difference is that in my previous dreams I was a young man, but in the one last night, I was old, more helpless than ever. I didn't share the dream with anyone, as I usually do. Not even with my wife.

Yes, I am retired, and no one comes to ask for my advice or seeks my approval any more, but I haven't stopped trying to keep up-to-date with government rules and Party lines. I feel I owe the government that much, but my family doesn't agree. Not long ago Loyal remarked to me that my brain has been washed by so much propaganda for so long that it's like a slab of granite. He was joined by my wife, who has, since we were married more than forty years ago, never contradicted me. The argument started as soon as the three of us stepped into the house after the village political meeting. The new Party secretary, whom I didn't recognize, re-emphasized the family-planning law and announced yet more severe penalties for any violation. His voice was firm and loud, tainted by an accent unfamiliar to my ears. But it was no way as powerful as the silence that followed. When the villagers were asked to stand up and voice their support and make personal promises, there was no response. Half an hour must have passed before I got to my feet and did my duty. That was the fuse that lit the home battle.

"You're retired," my wife, usually soft-spoken, shouted at me before the door was closed, tapping my temple with her fingers to suggest that I had lost my mind—a gesture she had never before made to me. "Why couldn't you keep your mouth shut like the rest? Haven't you learned that the lead bird takes the first bullet? What are you thinking, old man? Loyal is getting married in three months."

As if her words were not enough to teach me a lesson, she, for the first time since I took her for my wife, refused to cook me breakfast. She didn't get up the next day until lunchtime. As for Loyal, he didn't speak to me for a whole week.

I understood my wife's concern, and knew where Loyal's anger came from. I am a farmer, a peasant, good at planning crops. As for family planning, I find it even difficult to say these words. It's hard to follow, like many other rules and regulations. But I am aware that each year we have more and more people to feed. The statistics read to us at the meeting were no good to me. They are pushed into one ear and leave right away through the other. All I need is to walk around our village, go through our fields, and make comparisons. In our area, the land is not as rich and fertile as our southern neighbours', nor are our lakes and rivers as generous. Still we try to grow three crops a year instead of two, if weather permits. As soon as we bring in the spring wheat, we plant rice seedlings. When the harvested rice bundles are on the way to the threshing ground, the land is made ready for winter wheat to be sown. There is no spare season and our fields are never empty of labourers. Yet for the past two decades, our brigade, which I know the best, sometimes has to bring in grain grown somewhere else. We all work harder but in the end we still can't feed ourselves every year. And that's a bitter pill for a farmer to swallow. Over the past fifteen years the population in our village has doubled, but the arable land hasn't grown one inch.

I don't mind having fewer children around, to respond to the government call. But I must have a grandson of my own so that the spirit of the Chen family can live on. As long as I'm around, my family tree is not going to die.

LOYAL

(1980)

My father has told me often enough that he doesn't dislike *all* the changes that have taken place over the last two years, although some of them make him uneasy. I welcome them, because they have made my life a lot better than I ever imagined. For the first time I have come to realize that a farmer's standard of living doesn't have to be as tough and bitter as I was used to. And, believe me, I know what I'm talking about in that regard. Just look at the house we are living in now: a two-level building of real bricks, not a hut made from hard-packed mud mixed with chopped rice straw. It's true, we still have a thatched roof. We could have had clay tiles if my pathetic stab at private enterprise hadn't gone down the drain.

I grew up hearing about "Old Man Yu Moves the Mountain." In grade two I had to memorize the story for a school assignment. After that my father would ask me to tell it over and over again, to him alone and in front of guests, even to strangers. It didn't take long for me, my mother, and everyone else in our village to conclude that he was obsessed with the stubborn and unrealistic Yu. One thing has become clear to me: no matter what kind of spirit Old Yu was praised for, he could never build a house like ours by relying on his bare hands. He would have needed money. Moving dirt around wouldn't have brought him a cent, nor a piece of brick, with or without the god of heaven's generals. And that's the bottom line.

Nowadays, money means everything, much more than "correct thought;" even my old mama understands that. One of her favoured expressions is that the most capable wife can't make meals without a grain of rice. That's my mama, all right. She's an old-fashioned woman. I don't bother to tell her that not everyone in the world eats rice. Rich foreigners, I have learned, eat bread and meat instead. Mama would never believe me, particularly the daily meat part. She loves to reason things out by citing old sayings, which are plentiful in our region.

One of the first I came to know when I was a little kid at village school stated that if you had enough money, you could hire a ghost to do your work for you. At the time, our teacher, an old fragile man who didn't have any front teeth left, warned us that the adage was a "stinking bourgeois habit of thought." He had to write the saying on the blackboard because most of us couldn't understand what he tried to say, so confusing were the hisses and slurs mixed in with his words as he spoke through the wide space where his teeth had been. At home, my father told me sternly that there was no such thing as ghosts. Superstition and nonsense, he declared. I never repeated the saying again, but it stuck in my head.

Ever since the death of Chairman Mao, we have entered an era in which what was once right has become wrong, and previous error has turned to truth. The old adage began to make sense to me. Over a year ago our new leader, Deng Xiao-ping, declared to the whole nation that to be rich is glorious and so is making money on your own, the more, the faster, the better.

Since then I have often dreamed of getting rich. But I don't know how. One of my old man's mottoes is that being poor will make a person a better revolutionary. That particular gem, plus his madness over Old Man Yu, was the cause of his nickname, Old Revolutionary Chen. At sixty-five, he ought to enjoy what's left of his life, which anyone who has eyes can see is a lot better. But he had to involve himself in things that are no longer his concern. My wife, Chun-mei, claims that my father has too much time on his hands, that he is inventing his own way to kill it: first, to wind himself up tight over some issue, then unwind slowly. Mama says that the old man is looking for trouble with a lit lantern. She doesn't spell out what kind of trouble.

Lately, my father has become quiet, which is totally unlike him. He sits alone, his head hanging, his shoulders stooped, in the front room, our family's sitting and eating place. One long sigh is followed by a couple of short ones after he squeezes the lit end off his cigarette. His sudden mood change came after I told him that Chun-mei is pregnant, or as the locals would say, "bearing happiness."

How can I not know the reason behind his odd behaviour, being the only boy in the family? My father doesn't have wealth or property to pass on to me as foreigners do. He's never had a bank account. The purpose of his life, the struggles he has gone through, have been for one thing and one thing only: to have his name continue. He did his part, but because of the new government law allowing only one child per family, he is worried on my behalf. Yet he doesn't want to tell me what's troubling him, as if admitting his concern will cause Chun-mei to have a girl for sure.

Since Deng Xiao-ping's economic reforms began—I have adored Deng the way my father worshipped Chairman Mao—Father and I have been like opposite electric charges: when one touches the other, an explosion is the result. We argue over everything, like rebuilding our house and adding a second floor as most village families have done, after I was able to borrow money from the commune's credit union. All in all, he has been against almost everything I want to do.

"This same building has housed four children and two adults," he shouted when I first mentioned the renovation. "Your sisters left home with no missing legs or arms. How can you say now we need more space?"

We started construction anyway because my father is retired and the responsibility for the house and loan is mine, though the land where the house stands remains the property of the government. My father nearly choked when I told him that all three rooms on the second level were for the use of my new family. We would have a bedroom, a sitting room, and a nursery.

"Even *you* can't be in two places at the same time, can you?" he railed, following me from room to room. "When you sit in your *living room* you can't be lying in your bedroom. So, educate me. What's the need of three rooms? If this isn't wasteful, what is?"

He calmed down a bit only when my mother dragged him into the nursery where I had painted the walls sky blue instead of pink, like the other rooms. He seemed pleased by that, declaring an end to that round.

My original plan was that my parents would live downstairs. I heard that's what foreigners and city people preferred. But my father insisted that he and Mama needed only one room, and that his decision was absolutely final. So their living room became a warehouse and storage area for tools, and the third room at the front turned into an eating and gathering place, with an eight-person square table in the centre, four wooden benches around it. To fill up the empty spaces, I added more benches against the walls. It reminded me of our village's meeting place, where the government documents are read to us and its policies are passed on. There is only one kitchen in our house, at the back, on the ground level. Among all my upgrades, the kitchen has scored poorest. I won't dare to compare it with the photo I saw in a magazine when I was buying paint in the town market. I know quality when I see it. Everything in the picture was smooth, shiny, and stylish. I would be laughing in my dreams if we could afford the city folks' gas burners and running water all in one room.

Half our kitchen is taken up by a brick stove, waist-high, with a back wall that rises to the ceiling. Behind the wall is a small chamber, big enough for one person to sit on a low stool and feed knotted rice or wheat straw into the fuel channels in the back of the stove. There is no shining cookware in sight. The smoke changes everything to the colour of ash. We use pig-iron woks for every task: cooking rice, stir-frying vegetables, making soup, boiling water.

In the past, to devote space to a bath hut would have been an outrageous extravagance. A chamber pot was all we had. We bathed in a wooden tub placed in the room where we ate and slept. When I was a kid, the Liu River was my bathtub as soon as summer arrived, but in winter, even thinking about washing in the river gave me goosebumps. I would stop having baths altogether. Only those who had money to burn, as my old man would say, could afford to have a soak in the public bath pool six miles away. I myself have never set foot in the place.

Our bath hut, built in the corner of the backyard beside the well, is my own design. There is no flush toilet so far; I haven't laid eyes on one around here. The hut is about six by ten feet, divided into two sections. Our tub, a giant pig-iron wok, is set into a raised platform, and under it is a fuel channel, connected to the other room, which is big enough for one person to sit and feed straw into the fire.

The bath-house plan was one of the longest battles I fought with my father. His surrender finally came after my mother took my side. She added her voice to my threat that in the marriage market nowadays, with no fancy furniture or facilities, it would be difficult to find a good match for me. No sooner was this settled than a new clash broke out after I had my first bath. My father refused to let me dump the soapy water. He insisted that he and my mother would use the same water. "Such wastefulness of fuel and water will be punished by the God of Earth," he bawled, forgetting his hatred of superstition and blocking the entrance with his long arms. Like a warrior guarding a king's castle, he claimed the prize that time.

Among all our disputes, my campaign to start a business for my own profit was the most drawn-out and bitter. I would hate to admit that it was this battle that "broke my horns" as Chun-mei later put it. I didn't agree, but in reality I seldom fought with my old man after that.

The war broke out shortly after I was matched with Chun-mei. I received a second loan from the credit union, on top of what I owed for rebuilding the house. My father became apoplectic when I told him my idea.

"You're going to spend it on *rabbits?*"

"Yes. I have a plan. Put your heart at rest. The plan is foolproof and easy."

"How many did you buy?"

"Three pairs of white, one of black, and one of chocolate brown."

He became hysterical "Are you out of your mind? Are the damn things made of gold?"

That was exactly what I had demanded of the breeder after he told me the price. He reminded me airily that what I was looking at were no ordinary rabbits. "They are *English* angora rabbits, you idiot! If you can't afford them, there are plenty of people I can sell to."

Although to him I was a *Tu-bao-zi*—a dirt head—I knew the weight of the word *English*. Commodities that have

English letters printed on them are at a premium, no matter what the letters say. Most of us can't read them, anyway. It costs more if undershirts are labelled as T-shirts. In the town market, I have seen people wearing sunglasses with labels full of tiny letters still glued to the lenses. They look like fools, but they're in style.

The rabbits might not be pure gold, but their hair was, I told my father. I also flashed him the new information I had learned hours earlier, that in the world market, where China provided ninety-five percent of the mohair, one ounce of angora-rabbit hair sold for six U.S. dollars! Although I had never seen what a U.S. dollar looked like, I knew its value. It was not just that American money was worth much more than our yuan; there was no way we could get hold of it. After labouring in the fields all year round, with my face towards the earth and my back to the sky, I felt like dancing when I was handed more than a hundred yuan at the end of the year, and that was after deductions for my share of grain, fuel, fertilizer, and farm tools. Six U.S. dollars is what a city worker earns in a month if he's lucky, and equivalent to twice what I make in three. As I stared down at the skinny rat-like baby rabbits resting in my palms, I visualized balls of fluffy hair rolled into stacks of ten-yuan bills.

"One ounce of its hair is worth fifty yuan," I announced, raising my whole hand, all my fingers open wide. "And each rabbit can be harvested five or six times a year. All we have to do is to feed them when they are hungry, let them rest when they are tired. All they are required to do is to grow hair, tons of it. Then we just laugh and sing all the way to the credit union. It won't be long before we will join the ranks of Ten-thousand-yuan Family."

The ten-thousand-yuan family was one of Deng Xiaoping's new inventions in rural areas. Even the thought of seeing such a large amount of money made my head spin. I had no idea how anyone could be worth that much. The largest note in China was a ten, which was about one month's spending money for an ordinary family. I had to use pen and paper to work out how many ten-yuan bills these families had altogether. But nothing was more shocking than what I found out later: not only were ten-thousand-yuan families rich, they were treated as celebrities in our country, publicly praised by the government. I read about them in newspapers and heard about them through radio broadcasts. They were getting the same kind of attention and glory that used to be given to the poor when Chairman Mao was in charge.

Besides working in the fields, I had raised pigs, goats, and cows, and was rather good at it. Older and more mature, I just couldn't see myself unable to look after ten rabbits. They only ate grass. Raising them, or rather their hair, would be as easy as eating a bowl of rice.

After they spent the first night in a wooden cage in our backyard, I had to bring all the rabbits into the house the next day because, during the night, one of them was bitten to death by a yellow weasel. I set them up royally on the second floor, in the new bedroom-to-be. I further learned that if I wanted to have high-quality hair, the rabbits must be kept in a dust-free and noise-free environment. So the "emperor's relatives" as my father called them ended up sleeping on the new bed before Chun-mei and I had a chance to use it, protected by a mosquito net, while I made do with a mat on the cement floor. I checked them before I went to bed and looked them over first thing after I got up. With a bamboo ruler in hand, I measured the length of their hair, day after day, week after week. Everything about them grew, their bodies, their heads, their legs, but not their hair.

When summer arrived with some days over 33 degrees Celsius, I found myself riding my bike for over a mile to get blocks of ice to cool the cages and prevent the rabbits from expiring from heat. No one in my family nor anyone in the village had ever received such royal treatment. In those days I tried to avoid my parents, my father in particular. I was tired of seeing him shake his head and roll his eyes. For the first time in my memory, he was speechless, which I would have called a miracle under different circumstances. I kept telling myself that I couldn't risk my "investment," a new word I heard often. If I could not make a profit, at least I was going to break even. I had to. I needed the money. That was the bottom line.

Of the nine rabbits that escaped the weasel's teeth, not all of them died at once. Four succumbed to the heat—a rotten irony, since they still had short hair. But the final five gave me great joy when, at the morning measuring, I noted their hair was lengthening. Although the advance was small, my hope soared and once again I saw myself surrounded by piles of money. With each passing day their hair grew.

In my former life I must have been a fox or a weasel, the enemy of angora rabbits. One evening as I arranged the mosquito net over my little money-makers I noticed their hair was patchy and rough. Two days later they were all dead. The vet told me they died from massive blockage of their intestines. The rabbits had been chewing and eating their own hair! They preferred to die from swallowing their coats rather than give me a chance to be rich. I was too upset to harvest the remaining hair from the deceased rabbits; I buried them with their precious coats still on.

My father would have killed me if I were not his only son. I was certain of it. I heard such an earful of I-told-you-so's, I swore I would never utter those words as long as I lived.

The truth was, although I was sick and tired of being poor, lately I found it harder to live an improved life while some farmers, our neighbours, who had been as poor as the rest of us, became richer. They were building fancy houses, twice as big as ours, with clay roof tiles, large windows with metal frames, and wooden floors in each room. Some could afford meat every day; some even had savings accounts in the credit union. How could I not want to be a part of it? I wanted to have money so that I could have a wedding like the one held for the son of the rabbit breeder, giving banquets, lighting off fireworks while the bride and groom paraded through the village in a motorcar. When they married, all my sisters had was a trip in a donkey cart to the registration office in the commune where the bride and groom were issued two pieces of paper, declaring them husband and wife. I wanted more for my wedding, but my dreams died with the rabbits.

My father wants a grandson more than I want to have a son of my own. That's pretty much all he has hoped and lived for, even though he's never said as much. I was too young to remember the details of my two sisters who died from hunger at the age of eight and nine during the famine years. When I was older, I had to try very hard not to think about what had become obvious to me: that my survival, as a skinny, weak five-year-old, was associated with their agonizing death from starvation.

I had been a weak baby, said my mother, and I was called a sick duck by the villagers behind my parents' back. Out of old-fashioned superstition I was raised as a girl until I was eight. The belief was that a boy child attracted devils, and a sickly boy made the allure much stronger. Accordingly, throughout my childhood I was dressed in a girl's outfit, wearing clothes of printed fabric; my hair was let grow long and braided in two pigtails. All this was to pull the wool over devils' eyes, although I wondered many times even then how the devils could be so stupid, unable to see what ordinary farmers could. But in the eyes of my parents the plan worked because I lived and the devils took the lives of my two sisters instead. I had long stopped thinking that my survival and my sisters' death was a deadly see-saw game. As I got older I came to understand that sometimes in life sacrifice is necessary. My parents did their part so our family tree wouldn't cease to grow, and I was their hope, the seed. Now my wife is pregnant, and I, for the first time in a long, long while, find myself thinking once again about my two dead sisters. I can't bear to let their death mean nothing, and I won't.

CHUN-MEI

(1980)

If Chairman Mao were still alive, I could never have become the daughter-in-law of a Party official like Old Revolutionary Chen. In Mao's time our two families were as different as water and fire. Even if we had both been water we would have come from separate sources, as my mother would say. Loyal's family would be well water, sweet and pure, while mine would be muddy, black ditch water. Black was the colour that stained us. In the years of absurdity—my term for the Cultural Revolution—our doors and window frames were painted black by the Red Guards, in contrast to those of the pure "red" families like Loyal's.

The government included my family in the hated land-lord class five years before I was born. The Land Reform movement in 1950 confiscated all private land, including ours, the Ma family's, and redistributed it among the farmers in our village.

My father should never have accepted his inheritance when his father died. He had said it so often that, as a child, I wished Grandfather, who died one year before the Communists took power in 1949, would come out of his grave and take the land back with him. At other times, my father murmured that if only the family's land had been one-third of an acre less, we would have fallen into the rich peasant class, which was less contemptible. His regret was contagious. More than once, I desired with all my heart that somehow the government had made a mistake in measuring our land, and because of the error, before the entire village, the official would declare that we Mas were no longer members of the landlord class. When my wish didn't come true, I, too, stopped hoping and dreaming altogether.

I was the third child of four in my family, my parents' only girl. From the day I was born everyone in our village called me "the landlord's daughter," as if that was my name. I do have a real name, a very beautiful one according to my mother, because she chose it. Chun-mei means Spring Plum-blossom. My mother also said that it was not just a proper name for a girl but a true reflection of the time of my birth. "Spring had arrived," she recalled, "and the plum trees were in bloom."

But that was not what my father remembered. He claimed that the spring of 1956 was the coldest season he had ever experienced. "The temperature dropped so low that two cows belonging to the village's cooperative froze to death in the barn. If there were any blossoms, they were *dong-mei*, flowers on winter plum trees. Since you are our first girl, I let your mother pick a name for you as we had agreed earlier. Your mother has always hated the winter. Besides, to give her credit, the calendar did say that spring had officially arrived."

In my life, controversies such as this are like wheat ears after a harvest: they can be found everywhere. The name of our village comes to mind first. It houses around fifty families, and is called Yangshu Zhuang—Poplar Tree Village. But unlike Loyal's Liuhe Village, where the River Liu runs through its east end, our community's title is a misnomer: there was not a single tree in sight when I was growing up, poplar or any other kind. According to my eldest brother, Gen-fa, there used to be many tall trees around before I was born. "They lined the ox-cart paths and encircled the fields and houses," he told me. "Some were so straight and tall they resembled the clay generals guarding the village temple. It was during the Great Leap Forward, shortly after you were born, that all the trees were chopped down and fed into pathetic, jerry-built furnaces to make steel."

But no controversy in the entire world would be as big, as shocking, and as unexpected as having Loyal and me tie the knot.

He and I were put together by a matchmaker. The revival of matchmaking had very little to do with the sweeping changes blowing across the country. The matchmaking business, though criticized as old-fashioned and banned by the government for as long as I could remember, never really vanished. Even as a child I knew that if the political wind got stronger and the waves became higher, the matchmakers just went underground, and once the political storm passed over, they were back in business. To replace the practice, the government called upon young people to pursue freedom in love and marriage. Our village was sent a few propaganda posters. One of them, which I still remember vividly, showed a smiling young man and woman holding hands and looking up into an empty sky. In real life such freedom didn't exist, not when China was ruled by the emperors, nor under the thumbs of the warlords, the Nationalists, or the Communists. My great-grandfather didn't meet his bride, a daughter in the court of the Qing dynasty, or even see her face until his wedding night. The union of my parents, a landowner's son and a daughter of an equivalent family, was the product of the tradition in their time. When it was my two elder brothers' turn, a few years ago, they, too, had no choice but to marry girls of equal social status. There was nothing they could do or say. I spotted tears of joy in my father's eyes after the matchmaker confirmed that my second sister-in-law-to-be was from a rich peasant-class family. On their wedding day, my father congratulated Second Brother, calling him a lucky young man who had "landed on a higher branch."

Until the doughy-faced matchmaker showed up at our door on Labour Day, May the first, 1979, the thought of leaving my home and parents had little room in my mind. I had long since learned to appreciate the walls of our house. They might not have looked like the strongest barricades in the world, made from mud mixed with chopped hair and straw, but in my eyes they were my Great Wall, dividing the world into two parts. The world of yin, outside the wall, treated me and my family with endless humiliation and insult. It was a world of bullies who exercised "the dictatorship of the proletariat" over us, under which both my parents and my brothers were as powerless as I. The world of yang was behind our closed doors, when my parents became our mom and dad and we were their dear children. And being the only girl alongside three boys, I had more than my share of their love and care. Though I had passed the marriage age set by the government, I was not in a rush to leave my world of yang behind. For every girl, her final destination, whether she likes it or not, is the home of her husband. In our region and culture, marriage doesn't have a good reputation among brides. A daughter-in-law's life is described as suffering "under the thumb of her mother-in-law." As one saying has it, on her wedding day, the new bride is already looking forward to the moment eighteen years later when, if she is lucky enough to have a son, she herself becomes a mother-in-law so that she is able to terrorize her daughter-in-law.

My parents had never said one word, not so much as a hint about trying to get rid of me as most parents in the village would do as soon as their daughters turned twenty. Some parents are in such a hurry you'd have thought that if their daughters stayed at home one day longer they would spoil, like vegetables. It's particularly so among the families where, if they can find a way to spend one penny twice, they will: their daughters are heavy burdens. We girls, from the time we are born, are called *Pei-qian-huo*—money-losing items, or bad investments, a term I often hear Loyal mimic. Our parents feed us and bring us up, but in the end it's the families of our husbands who reap the benefit. The earlier we are matched and married off, the more money and food can be saved. In the past few years, as I eyed the matchmakers darkening my neighbours' thresholds and watched girls my age and younger leave the village one after another, I pictured myself, "the girl of a landlord," as a high mountain that sat on my parents' shoulder, heavier than the ones that blocked Old Man Yu's house. I doubted there were any young men around who wanted me for a wife.

The unexpected appearance of Sister Liu changed all that. The chubby woman, with one eye bigger than the other, charged into our house, smiling and obsequious. "Your girl must have done something virtuous in her former life," she crowed.

My parents stood inside, at the doorway, dumbfounded.

"You will never guess who has sent me to talk about the happy matter of your daughter." She paused, not for an answer, only to suck in a mouthful of air. "Not in one hundred years!" she declared, letting out a hoarse laugh, pushing past my parents. "It's Secretary Chen! The Party bigwig!" Her voice dramatically went up one scale. She marched towards my father's old rattan chair and sat down, looking up at my parents. I stood at the back of the house, leaning against the kitchen door, watching the developments with great interest.

"Secretary Chen has chosen Chun-mei to be his son's wife. His only son, Loyal." The matchmaker suddenly held up her hands, forming a chubby knot in front of her lumpy chest, her eyes half closed, the smaller one a thin line. She appeared drunk on her own words.

"Oh, god of heaven, I've been in this business for many years but I never have pulled off a match like this. Nor did my mama, I'm sure. Not since the Emperor Qin united

China. You can only imagine how shocked I was. At first I thought I had heard him wrong. I had to ask Secretary Chen twice to make sure that it was your girl he was talking about. Times must have changed!" So saying, she gave such a whack on her raised knee that I was certain she hurt herself.

Secretary Chen was no stranger to me and my family. He had been one of the most important and powerful men in our area, as I had been reminded most of my life. After his retirement, we saw less of him, but once in a while his name was still mentioned. Liuhe Village is about four miles south of us. I had never paid any more attention to him than I did to other higher-ups, but my father had a different opinion. He once said that, unlike some of the Party bosses, Secretary Chen had earned his glory by the calluses on his palms.

In the years when political rallies and meetings were as numerous as hairs on an ox, Secretary Chen made frequent visits to our village, which was a part of his jurisdiction. On each occasion, he reminded us of his importance, not by making long and boring speeches as most leaders did but by his physical appearance. He was the tallest man I had ever seen. On the stage, he always sat in the centre seat of the front row, so his six-foot-two frame and door-wide shoulders could not be missed. It was an open secret that Secretary Chen had "word blindness." In other words, he was illiterate. Thus, making speeches and reading documents or newspaper articles to the audience was something he avoided. I had never talked to him, and was glad for it. I feared almost all officials. The bigger ones made me even more afraid. I had no idea Chen had known about me.

From the moment Sister Liu descended on our home, I didn't know what to think. Was I supposed to feel flattered, not just remembered by such an important person but sought after? When I had calmed down, there was only one question left. "Why me?"

Throughout her visit, Sister Liu had ignored me. I was standing no more than five feet away from her and caught her looking in my direction a few times. But it appeared my parents didn't feel slighted. After they saw the matchmaker off, they seemed to be relieved.

If my mother and father had ever harboured worries that their only daughter was going to be an old maid, the clouds had parted. I examined my father's thoughtful face as he headed to the bedroom, and I wondered what was going through his mind. Was he imagining my climb up a ladder with the possibility of becoming the daughter-in-law of a Party official? Would he tell me that unlike my brother, who only got on a higher branch, I was going up all the way to the treetop?

I had learned at an early age that hoping makes life hard to live. But sometimes I couldn't help myself. I didn't get as much education as I would have liked. I was in grade four when the Cultural Revolution shut down every school across the country. In opposition to government policy, my parents taught me and my younger brother to read and write at home after darkness fell, when our front door was closed and braced with a tree post so that no one could barge in as they did so often during the day. When it came to educating us children, my parents seemed to have bundles of energy. Among the many things I learned, one thing stood out remarkably well in my understanding: human beings searched relentlessly for other people to look down upon.

In a country as large as China, it appeared to my young mind that there was no room for peace—never mind love and care—for my family, particularly my father. The constant political movements left no harmony. We were at the bottom of the social ladder. On a wider scale, city folks ridiculed farmers, even though we counted for eighty percent of the population. Yet the discrimination didn't stop there. Among city people, those living in big urban areas like Shanghai or Beijing felt superior to the ones in smaller cities. Among the farmers in our village, the poor peasants despised those who were rated as middle class, who in turn looked down upon the upper-middle class. Geography also came into play. The farmers who made homes on the southern shore of the Yangtze River, the region known as the land of fish and rice, jeered at us on the northern side of the river. When it came down to our region, every inch became accountable. The farther north we were, the less valuable we became. If a young woman married into a family south of where she had lived, her social status was elevated, but if a young man ended up with a wife who came from even a few miles to the north, he and his family would lose face.

So by noon on the day of Sister Liu's visit, the news of my proposed match had spread across the village. Those who came to see my parents all said one thing. "Your girl has hit a double jackpot."

According to a local saying, a perfect couple possesses *lang-cai-nui-mao*—groom's intelligence and bride's good looks.

Loyal and I met once before our wedding day, six months after Sister Liu's first visit, so I had little opportunity to find out the quality of his brain. But he seemed to like my looks, and told me so. I am not beautiful, not even close, but I have very pale skin, which is considered beauty itself by the locals. My eyes are large, like my mother's, and I have folded eyelids. They too are a much-sought-after feature in females. In the years of chaos, my pale skin, believe it or not, was cited as a bourgeois trademark. The propaganda posters said so. All the heroes and heroines held up to us as models had bronze-hued skin, while discredited leaders and the American imperialists had a white, ghost-like look. Many times, my skin was burned and even blistered after working in the paddies under the scorching sun, yet I wasn't allowed to wear a straw hat like the rest. The village leaders wanted my skin to darken. But there was nothing they could do when I turned pale again as winter arrived. Nowadays, though, my natural colour is prized again.

Loyal is a pleasant-looking man. But he sure is a chatterbox. I didn't tell him that. During our first meeting, all he did was talk, about the weather, crops, his plans, and his family. He must have taken after his mother. Unlike his father, who is tall and strong, a typical man of Shandong, Loyal is no more than five foot four, a bit shorter than I. He complained that his "under-development" was caused by years of shouldering heavy loads. I enjoyed his frankness, and his sense of humour was rare to my ears.

From him I also confirmed my lingering suspicion that my becoming the object of his father's attention might have had a lot to do with duck eggs.

Around that time, a Hong Kong businessman named Wang had paid a visit to my father. Wang, a middle-aged, stiff-necked man, turned up in a fancy car, accompanied by the important leaders of our commune. For days it was the most talked about event in the village. To me, the whole thing was as surprising as a thunder on a cloudless day.

In the book of the government, my family had been marked down as the landlord class for three generations. The truth was that my ancestors had become rich first and landowners later. Their wealth came not from crops but from producing the area's most famous salted duck eggs. The highly saline-alkaline soil in our region was one of the reasons for their success.

My great-grandfather had started the business. By the time my grandfather passed away, the salted eggs were not only well known locally, they were shipped all over Southeast Asia. In the 1940s, when the Nationalists were in power, there were regular shipments to President Chiang Kai-shek, whose love for salty food was no secret.

"Our business was the envy of every farmer on the south bank of the Yangtze," my father had once told me. "The ones who look down on us as ignorant northerners. In fact, they were working for us. Since they have more lakes and rivers than our roads, they raised the ducks and sent the eggs to me. For years, they tried to copy our recipe and produce the eggs themselves, but with no success." That all happened before I was born. When I was growing up, I hardly saw any ducks or eggs around. The government had denounced and banned all non-farming practices in the countryside. Any kind of business was "growing a capitalist tail."

From what I had gathered from my father, high-quality salted eggs must come from ducks; chicken eggs are no good. Each egg had to be washed before it was dipped in a thick paste, a mixture of dirt, vermilion dye, and spices. The spices were the key ingredient and my family's closely guarded secret. The coated eggs were then placed in clay jars, sealed, and stored for a certain period of time, depending on the season. The warmer the temperature, the less time it took for the eggs to cure. When they were ready, the paste was washed off and the eggs were boiled or steamed. Most people liked to cut the cooked egg in half, still in the shell, serve it as a cold dish, or eat it with rice porridge.

The elegantly dressed Mr. Wang wept when he was introduced to Father. He held my father's hands for a long time before letting them go, choking on his words as he described how his own beloved father had missed the salted duck eggs. Wang had searched all over Hong Kong for eggs that would meet his father's taste, but the old man was never satisfied.

The meeting with Wang was the first time in my life that I saw my father given respect and praise in public. What a wonderful yet strange feeling that was! Before his departure, Mr. Wang persuaded my father to go into business with his company, to make salted duck eggs again, in the old way.

Although all the lights of bureaucracy turned green, the business, as expected, had a very slow start. After three decades of concentration on grain crops, it was hard to find duck eggs in quantity. Even a kid can tell you that with no eggs there will be no ducks, and without ducks, no eggs. A few weeks before my wedding, about eight months after

Mr. Wang's visit, the first truckload of duck eggs arrived in our village.

Secretary Chen must have got wind of Mr. Wang's visit and figured out that the wheel of my family's fortune was about to turn. Loyal confirmed my suspicion. Although I appreciated his honesty, I couldn't help tasting bitterness. Even worse was something else Loyal told me. His father had favoured me over other young women because my mother had given birth to three boys and only one girl. Secretary Chen assumed I was like my mama, inclined to bear male children. He was so much under the control of this ridiculous stupidity that he brushed aside the gossip whispered in the village that I had a rebellious streak.

"Once married," Loyal mimicked his father, "headstrong or not, your wife will have to defer to me and to you, and later to her son."

I was aware of the theory of bloodlines, which says that the dragon's son is a dragon and the offspring of a mouse is born with the talent to dig holes. But Loyal's father was way off line on this nonsense, and the tradition dictating that my marriage to Loyal would absorb me into his family did nothing to dissolve my sadness and resentment. My father-in-law chose me for possible business connections and breeding, the way he might select a farm animal.

The news that I was "bearing happiness" swooped through the Liuhe Village as if it had wings. It was what Loyal's family, my father-in-law in particular, had anxiously awaited since the wedding two months before. The humming and buzzing reminded me once again of the stern reality that the

Chen family's continuation required a son of a son. And my duty was to meet the demand. Every single eye in the village would be on my swelling belly, and my head already felt heavy with worry.

"I have only one son." It was one of my father-in-law's frequent laments over cups of warmed rice wine, when he was inside the walls of his house. "Who will pass on my family's spirit if I don't have a grandson?"

Loyal may be the head of the family in many ways since his father's retirement, but when it came to the child I am bearing, my husband lost his voice right then and there. True, Loyal treated me with respect. But if I had hoped to be the moon to his sun, my expectation turned to bubbles when he mentioned to me one night that he owed his loyalty first to his father, second to his mother, then to the memory of his two sisters. I came fourth. Secretary Chen has raised his son well.

One fine spring evening, when the sun had almost vanished below the horizon, illuminating the western sky with golden rays, I was reminded yet again that my life and body were no longer my own. After we sat down for supper, my father-in-law said to Loyal, "I went to see Old Fu this morning. He has agreed to examine your wife tonight."

I blushed, quickly lowering my head, putting down my chopsticks. I stared at my bowl of rice, my fingers linked together on my lap, the knuckles turning white. I began to tremble.

"Yes, Father," Loyal answered, his mouth jammed full, his jaws moving determinedly, his eyes avoiding me. "We'll go to Lao Fu straight after the meal."

"We must know," my father-in-law mumbled again, filling up his wine cup. "Chairman Mao taught us that to go into a war unprepared was to be defeated."

"Know what?" I heard myself ask. I had always recognized the significance of my baby's gender, but I had never expected the birth to be compared to a war. What kind of battle was he talking about? And who was his enemy? I sat dumbfounded, hardly touching my food as the others consumed theirs in silence.

As the night deepened, we left the village. I followed Loyal across the dry paddy dikes, over a stone bridge, along a hard-packed dirt road, heading to the Fu Family village where Lao Fu—Old Fu, Wicked Fu, or "Mr. Wind and Water"—lived. I had never met Fu in person but had heard plenty about him in the past few years after he resumed his old practice. His business, inspired by his so-called talent, or heaven-given gifts as he boasted, ranged from selecting appropriate burial sites for the dead to determining the most auspicious location of new buildings. Like many old habits and traditions that had been condemned by the government as spreading superstition, Fu's services were in great demand. But I had no idea that Wicked Fu had acquired a new skill, forecasting the gender of fetuses.

If I had had no grudge against him, Fu would have appeared to be a grandfatherly-looking man. He had a broad face, and round eyes that were sharp and alert despite puffiness and wrinkles. His thin white hair was combed back but refused to stay in that position long. He shook hands with Loyal, nodding and smiling politely in my direction. He looked me over carefully but avoided my eyes.

Wicked Fu offered us tea. He didn't insist after Loyal shook his head and said no. Loyal and I had been travelling in silence ever since we left home. His no-discussion attitude filled me with sadness. I would have loved a cup of tea to ease my nerves.

"I'm honoured that your father has entrusted me with his own son although my poor skills may be inadequate," Fu said to Loyal with accustomed false humility. The old man might have wasted no time catching up with the new trend of making money, but he seemed to have failed to update himself that false modesty was also on the way out as changes rushed in.

No wonder Loyal frowned. He seemed about to say something but decided against it.

"Perhaps your esteemed wife would lie down here," Fu went on, pointing to a raised brick platform that took up a corner of the small room: an old-fashioned, peasant-style bed. No one was talking to me, so I had a chance to look around. Apart from a three-legged desk beside the bed, the room was bare of furniture. A stack of bricks had been used to replace the missing leg. On the wall beside the desk was a small medicine cabinet with a red cross painted on the door, which reminded me of the village clinic where my pregnancy had been confirmed.

I walked to the brick bed, which was covered by a thin, grey quilt, as uninviting as the rest of the place, and lay down on it. The bed was cold and hard against my back, as if I was lying in a grave.

"When I was in the city last year, I heard of this method people use in the West," Fu said to Loyal. "I was skeptical at first, but after I tried it a few times, I am pleased to tell you that the method is foolproof. Now, if your wife will kindly bare her abdomen."

With a tenderness that was unusual for him, Loyal unbuttoned my shirt a few inches from the hem to reveal my stomach. When he reached to undo my trousers I grabbed his hands.

"A palm-width below the navel will suffice," Fu instructed, stern faced. "This is no time for her to be modest."

I watched Loyal move away, until I could no longer see him. I then clamped shut my eyes but quickly opened them again. I took a deep breath, drawing into my lungs the stale odours around me—cooking oil, coal smoke, and dampness. Beside me, the old man stood, leaning on the edge of the bed, threading a needle with his bony fingers.

"It's as simple as it is accurate." He turned to Loyal, clearing his throat noisily. "If the needle rotates to the right, it's a boy; if to the left"—he shrugged—"then your esteemed wife may have to pay a visit to the clinic. Now—" he paused for a second, "let's see."

Pinching one end of the cotton thread between the thumb and finger of his right hand, Old Fu held the needle above my lower abdomen. I lifted my head as far as I could while trying to keep my body still, and watched him clasp the thin thread with the thumb and index finger of his left hand, drawing downward to the needle to steady it before he let it go.

Three pairs of eyes locked on the tiny needle. It hung motionless for a second, then slowly began to rotate.

"The needle has turned right! It's a male!" Loyal exclaimed, joy in every word. "Isn't that so?"

"Yes. Yes," the Wind and Water man responded, winding the thread around his finger. "Your father will be pleased."

"And generous, too, Old Fu," Loyal added. "Your service to our family will be rewarded."

Fu showed us out, an unctuous smile plastered across his face.

As we made our way home, Loyal chattered cheerfully on, as if a heavy load had been suddenly lifted off his shoulders. "I am going to have a son, a grandson for my father. All the sacrifices have finally paid off."

My mind, meanwhile, was miles away. From where I had lain I had had a clear view of the old man's hand. Just as he released the needle he had almost imperceptibly turned it to the left, ensuring the hoped-for sign.

Listening to Loyal talk on and on about the past and future, I didn't have the stomach to tell him what I had seen. Revealing Fu's stunt would cause turmoil, and I wanted peace.

PART THREE

Milford, Ontario

JANE

(June 1989)

Friday is usually Kevin's day to mow the grass. He comes home a bit early—there isn't much insurance business on Fridays—and puts on his work clothes, does the lawns, and putters about in the garden until dinner. That way the outside chores are done and his weekend is free. He hasn't gone into the office on a Saturday for years.

So when I called the girls to the table for a supper of barbecued veggie burgers, chicken breasts, and roast corn on the cob, Kevin was relaxed and refreshed after a hot shower and enjoying a pre-dinner cocktail on the patio. Megan was in a grouchy mood, having spent a beautiful afternoon working frantically on an English essay, which was, if I knew her, late; and Dong-mei was chirpy, since it was her weekend to command the television.

As soon as we sat down the phone rang. As usual, Kevin suggested we let the answering machine pick it up, and as usual we ignored him. Dong-mei jumped to her feet and grabbed the phone.

"Oh, hi, Grandpa," she said cheerily as a sour look passed over her face. "Hold on. Mom's right here." And she tossed the cordless phone to me as if it was a hot iron.

Neither of my daughters liked to talk to my father on the phone. Megan and Dong-mei enjoyed Dad's company and his stories, but they tried to avoid one-on-one occasions with him, when, they complained, the librarian in him shuffled out of its cave. He meant well, but sometimes he turned the conversation into an interrogation about school, unsatisfied with vague answers like "okay" or "fine." He would ask Megan what she was reading, then quiz her about the book. He questioned Dong-mei about books he had bought for her or loaned her. Poor Dong-mei. At eight she had no sophistication to fend him off gently. She would admit that she forgot where she had left the unread books.

Dad's call was abrupt for him. "Turn on the TV," he said. "Right away. It's about China. Talk to you later." I got up from the table and went into the family room with the phone still in my hand.

"Mom," Dong-mei yelled from the table. "Supper's not over yet."

She couldn't resist the jab. Our firm rule was, no TV until supper was finished and the dishes cleared away. Kevin says I have a thing about families that eat in front of the TV, or don't have meals together at all—and he's right.

On the TV screen was a photo of a cityscape.

"That's Beijing," Kevin said, leaning against the door jamb. "Tiananmen Square."

The girls followed him into the room.

"Nice going, Dad," Megan said. "It says so on the bottom of the screen."

"Why are we staring at some stupid picture?" Dong-mei grumbled. "This is a waste of time."

"Be quiet, Dong-mei," I said.

The girls were allowed an hour of TV per weekday, and they had to have a reason for watching a show; no sitting-and-surfing allowed. On alternate weekends, Megan or Dong-mei had first say in what we should watch. While Kevin and I had been weeding the flowerbeds, Dong-mei had regaled us with the lineup of shows she planned for the weekend, starting at eight o'clock that night. She was grumpy and impatient because she was afraid her plans were unravelling.

I wasn't surprised to see the report from Beijing. All spring, it seemed, I had been reading newspaper articles about growing student unrest in China, and when Russia's President Gorbachev paid his much-anticipated state visit to the capital city, press from around the world were there, and it wasn't long before they trained their cameras on the protesters who occupied Tiananmen Square. The still photo on the screen showed what looked like a vast, messy campground. It appeared more festive than threatening.

"This is boring," Dong-mei tried again. "A picture of buildings and crowds."

"Be patient," Kevin told her, sitting down in his favourite chair. "Jane, should we bring our supper in here?"

"Okay," I said, but, distracted by the commentary, I didn't move. The girls looked at each other in amazement.

"The protesters are trying to force the government to stop corruption in the Party," the reporter said. "The army has surrounded Beijing, waiting for the call to move in and clear them out."

"Hey, that's the Forbidden City in the background," Megan cut in. "We read about it in Politics this year. That's where the emperor and his family used to live. No one else could go in. Or something like that. Now it's open to tourists."

"Why can't those students stay where they want?" Dong-mei asked. "It's a free country, isn't it?"

"Grace, you can be *so* out of it sometimes," Megan replied in the superior tone she knew her sister hated. "China, a free country?"

Kevin said, "Let's hear what the reporter has to say, girls."

The journalist, whose photograph was on the screen—there was still no video—said that the students were highly organized and had been joined recently by factory workers. The government was raging mad because China had lost face in front of the entire world. As soon as Gorbachev had gone home the army had been called in.

"This looks bad," I murmured. "Dad says some China experts are predicting a civil war."

The photo was replaced by live video. Stiff-faced soldiers in olive drab, with bags criss-crossed on their chests and rifles in their hands, stood tightly packed together on the bed of a truck. The camera zoomed out to show a long line of trucks stretched down a wide avenue, swamped by a sea of people, women and men who looked as if they had been coming home from work or the market. The trucks weren't moving. A young woman climbed onto the front fender of one of the trucks and shook her fist, shouting something at the soldiers.

Another shot, this time showing the students massed in the square.

"How can the soldiers possibly move all the protesters out?" Megan asked. "Even if they *could* make it to the square?"

Dong-mei continued to fidget. Our supper grew cold in the kitchen. Finally, the voice on the TV announced, "We now return to our regularly scheduled program."

"Hooray!" Dong-mei shouted.

GRACE

❀

(June 1989)

Of all days, I liked Sunday best, especially in the morning, and I still do. It was the only time I could while away a few hours free from the watchful eyes and supervising ears of my parents and my big sister. I would wake up early and go downstairs in my PJs, park myself in the centre of the family-room floor or curl up in the leather easy chair, usually the turf of my father, and turn on the TV with the volume low because my parents' bedroom was also on the ground floor. As I watched my favourite shows, I would have a picnic—a bag of potato chips, some candies or a chocolate bar—content and master of the house.

This Sunday morning I checked the clock on the mantel as I passed the fireplace: ten past seven. I was up earlier than usual because my parents had stolen my TV time watching the news. I settled in the chair, pulled a blanket over myself, and turned on the TV, ready for some solitary quality time watching music videos, which were against the rules because I was "only eight and a half," as my sister loved to gloat. But no music could be heard, no rock stars pranced across the stage. A movie was playing instead. A murky evening sky filled the screen. A wide avenue, dimly lit by amber street lights. But this was no movie. It was Tiananmen Square again, and its tent city and confusion of people and buses and barricades. In the darkness, people running in all directions, fleeing in waves. Their fear and desperation were obvious. I turned the sound up a little and got out of the chair and onto my knees, close to the TV. Panicked screaming rose up, more real than any movie I had ever seen.

Then the street lights went out. The sudden darkness seemed to bump up the sound. I could make out the shadowy forms of thousands of people, a burning bus in the distance, then trucks and a tank moving quickly down the avenue as people dashed out of the way. A man and woman on a bike didn't make it. My stomach churned as the tank ran over them and sped on.

A second column of trucks appeared and soldiers spilled out of the backs, lining up in formation. More screams, more panic as people tried to run away. Then came the gunshots. The camera zoomed in on a white object that jerked and fell to the ground. The man or woman—I couldn't tell—lay twitching. A dark stain spread across the shirt front as the twitching slowed and stopped. More gunfire. More bodies hit the ground.

I was never so sure in my life that everything that appeared on the screen in front of me, the blood, the shouts, the gunshots, the bodies, and the death were as real as the screams I heard in my ears. My own screams.

"Mom! Dad! They're killing people!" I yelled, backing away from the TV. Suddenly the room shook with the deafening roar of the crowd, the hammering of machine-gun fire. I had fallen back on the remote and boosted the volume.

As I scrambled backwards from the horror on the screen, Mom and Dad rushed into the room, pulling their robes on. Dad picked up the remote and muted the TV, then turned it off.

"What the hell's going on?" he demanded.

"What have you been watching?" Mom said sternly.

"I don't know. It was the same place we saw last night," I told her, my voice shaking. "I didn't mean to see it, honestly. I wanted to watch my show. But they put something else on instead. A war."

I began to cry, still unable to believe or understand what I had seen. I hated fights and violence, real or acted. The sight of blood, mine or someone else's, sickened me. Killing or deaths on TV or in movies repelled me. What I had just seen was far worse; it was real.

"It sounds like live coverage from Beijing," Dad said quietly to Mom. "God. Murders on Sunday morning."

Mom put her arm around me. "Come on," she said gently, "let's go make some tea and we'll talk about it."

As soon as we left the room, I heard the TV go on again. When the tea was made and Mom and I were sitting at the kitchen table, Dad came in.

"It's on almost every channel," he said. "They're already calling it the Beijing Massacre."

Mom looked up at him and pointed her chin at me.

"I won't go into detail," he said.

"It was real gunfire, wasn't it, Dad?"

"Yes, it was."

"And all those people were really shot?"

He nodded.

"The army must have gone mad," Mom murmured, staring into the cup between her hands.

For the rest of the day I stayed away from the family room, on orders from my parents—unnecessary orders. Either Mom or Dad would be in front of the TV and would bring updates to the other. At noon, Megan got up, had her tea and toast while Mom told her about the events of the morning, and joined the "team" that monitored the reports.

I went up to my room for a while and tried to play with my dolls, changing them into different outfits, trying new hairstyles, but the images of what I had seen that morning kept pushing into my mind—the eerie red sky, the dim street lights and sudden darkness, the screaming people, so many of them, and their desperate attempt to escape the soldiers' bullets and the tanks. And on top of it all, the faces of the soldiers were just like my face. So were the faces of the victims.

Later on in the afternoon, I went outside and lay on the grass. It was pleasantly hot and the sky was clear blue. The image of the dead person in the white shirt slipped in and out of my mind, no matter how hard I tried to erase the memory of the blood-soaked clothes. What would the government say to the parents? I wondered.

Dad went into great detail with me after I asked him what was going on. He said that the government of China had labelled the demonstrators counter-revolutionaries. "It means they are enemies of the country, and their families are considered guilty, too."

"But they weren't doing anything wrong!" I protested. "I saw them. The soldiers attacked them! Do you mean the family of the person I saw killed are enemies now?"

"I'm afraid so. That's how it works over there."

"But it's not fair!" I said, tears coming to my eyes.

Dad lifted me onto his lap, something I hadn't let him do for a long time. He held me close to him and rocked the easy chair a little.

"Dad," I said a short while later, "is Yangzhou close to Beijing?"

"No, it's a long way south of Beijing. Why?"

"I was just thinking about those people you told me about, the ones who helped you and Mom adopt me."

"Oh, I'm sure they're okay," he said quietly. "They're a long way from . . . the event."

"What about Chun-mei?" I asked.

"I'm sure she's all right, too."

Our eyes met briefly. I looked away.

It was the first time I had said the name Chun-mei without anger.

A few days later Mom asked me if I wanted to go to the Chinese consulate in Toronto to take part in a ceremony to mourn the people who had been killed in Beijing. "It's the least we can do, to let the Chinese government know how we feel about what they did to their own people," she said.

I agreed. I liked the idea, and the way she asked me, which made me feel older and more mature.

In the days that followed, the June 4th Tiananmen Square Massacre was on the radio and TV day and night. I followed some of the reports. I wanted to know why it happened. Miss McKerrow, my teacher, talked about it in class. There were many protests, marches, and demonstrations all over the world, especially in Hong Kong, she said, pointing to a spot on the map.

In the halls, the teachers looked at me in a different way, and so did some of the kids. Did they blame me for what had happened? Did they sympathize with me? But why? I wasn't Chinese. They all knew that.

JANE

❀

(1990)

Megan called out, "Mom, no meat for me, please!"
"But you love barbecued chicken breast. Take a
little bit."

"No way," Megan persisted. "Do you know how many
growth hormones there are in chicken nowadays? Tons. We
learned about it in biology. All those chemicals can't be
good for us. And Amy says meat has cholesterol that makes
you fat."

"Yuck," said Dong-mei. "I don't want to eat chemicals!"

I shot Megan a look that she blissfully ignored. Kevin
helped himself to a second piece. "Maybe Megan is right,"
he suggested in his ironic tone. "She's only seventeen and
she's almost full-grown. And as for Grace, in a couple of
years she'll be the tallest in the family."

Megan had become almost obsessive about food lately,
since she had become friends with Amy, a girl as thin as a

stick who wanted to go into modelling. To Megan, growing seemed a sort of crime, and getting bigger was sinful. She had cut down on her meat intake, then asked me to do stir-fries with only bits of meat among the vegetables. I went along with her. I knew what she was afraid of. The hormone angle was just a ruse.

Kevin had put on some weight over the last few years. Nothing extravagant, but he had a bit of a belly now and a comfortable look about him that, frankly, I liked. But every time Megan passed him, it seemed, she'd pat him on the belly and offer some sarcastic remark. "When's it due?" or "Better cut down on the brews, Dad." Her snarky comments were a cover for her fear that she'd end up with a shape like her mother's.

The girls kid me sometimes because I'm just over five feet tall, especially since both of them passed me a long time ago. I'm narrow at the shoulder and wide in the hips—or, as Dong-mei put it tactlessly one day, pear-shaped. I came to grips with my oh-so-un-chic body a long time ago, after more than enough anguish as a teenager, but in my eldest daughter's eyes I see fear every time she looks at me.

"Well, relax, kids," Kevin went on. "It's your genes that will decide on your size, not what's put into chicken feed."

"What's genes?" Dong-mei asked, already forgetting her new fear of chemicals and selecting the biggest chicken breast on the platter.

"We studied that in biology, too," Megan said. "A gene is a unit of material inside our cells that's inherited from our parents. It controls what we look like and how smart we are and . . . stuff."

"Thanks," Dong-mei said. "Now maybe Dad can translate."

"Think of a gene as a little computer program that tells our bodies how to grow as we get older. We get the genes from our parents, as Megan said. The same number from each."

"So we can't choose them?"

"No, dumb-dumb, we're born with them," Megan answered.

"It's not as if our whole lives are decided ahead of time," I assured her. "Each of us was born an individual and we all have to work hard to be the person we want to be."

But I had missed the call entirely. Dong-mei put down her fork as tears welled up in her eyes. Kevin stopped eating and looked at me, eyebrows raised.

"All Megan has to do is look at you to see how she'll turn out," Dong-mei said quietly. "I got my genes from two people I've never met."

Kevin caught on right away. "Yes, dear, but—"

"I'm going to be ugly, then. Only ugly people would abandon their own baby."

GRACE

❀

(1990)

Winter meant skating, tobogganing, the holidays, and Mom's campaign to make sure Megan and I had no free time on our hands. In the past, she had always signed us up for crafts, sewing, swimming, skating, even French and Spanish lessons. Sure enough, one day I came home from school to find a pamphlet on the kitchen table, "Winter Made Fun." Dad sat there drinking tea from a mug, reading the paper.

"What's that?" I asked, my bag still on my shoulders.

"Oh," Dad said casually, looking at the glossy picture on the pamphlet, "your mom asked me to pick it up for you and Megan."

I poured myself a glass of milk and headed for the living room.

"At least have a look at it," Mom said later.

I whined; Megan complained. We weren't interested.

We were too busy. Everything they offered looked stupid and boring. Why couldn't our parents leave us alone?

Before I went to bed, she brought up the issue again. "There is one thing you could give a try, something entirely new."

Megan was in the hall, and this brought her to the door. "What?" she said.

"Well, I was thinking of Dong-mei."

"What is it?" I asked warily.

"I was talking to Frank last night on the phone," Mom began.

Frank Wu and my parents had become closer than ever since Tiananmen happened. He had come up to Milford on the bus a few times. When my parents were in the city, they'd have dinner with him.

"He's teaching Mandarin again this winter," Mom said. "In the north end of the city, half an hour's drive from here." She let the sentence hang. "Your dad would be willing to take you there two afternoons a week after school."

"I thought Frank spoke Chinese," Megan said.

I wished she would shut up and let Mom talk herself out. But no, she always had something to say.

"Mandarin is the official dialect in China," Mom explained.

"Is it easy to learn?" Megan asked.

Mom smiled. Here we go, I said to myself. "There's only one way to find out," Mom said.

"I think being able to speak Chinese would be neat," Megan bubbled. I wished I could stuff a sock in her mouth. I knew she'd quickly lose interest, like she always did.

"Forget it," I told my mother, silently cursing both of them, Megan in particular. Would Mother *ever* lay off trying to keep me in touch with my roots? "No way. I'm having enough trouble with French at school, even after those crummy lessons you made me take last winter. So leave me out of your *neat* plan," I said, glaring at my sister.

"You don't even want to give it a try, Dong-mei? If you don't like the lessons, you can always drop them. You've dropped out of things before," she added sweetly. "At least then you can say you tried."

I'd heard that last sentence so many times it was engraved in my memory, and I said it along with her in my head.

"And Frank is such a nice guy," Mom quickly added.

"Yeah," Megan said. "At least we'll know our teacher. Come on, Grace, you'd be able to write your own name in Chinese."

"So? Who cares?"

"In the spring you're going to study about China in school," Mom said, never giving up. "Wouldn't it be fun to know a little about the language? And you like Frank, don't you?"

"I want to try it," Megan said. "And don't forget, Grace, that in two weeks I take the test for my permanent driver's licence. If I pass, you and I can go to the city by ourselves."

Suddenly Megan's enthusiasm made sense.

"We'll have to see about that," Mom said doubtfully. "Anyway, Dong-mei, think about it, will you? If you take Chinese, your dad and I won't ask you to sign up for anything else, like piano lessons."

"Okay," I said. "If Megan can take me when she gets her licence." I could drive a bargain, too.

"It's a deal," Mom said, trying to hide a smile.

I took my lessons at the Hua Sheng—Voice of China—language school, above a store that smelled of rotten fruit and dead fish. I stuck with it for the first year, after wavering a bit in March, when Mom hinted that it was either Chinese or piano lessons. I hoped that, after the break for summer holidays, I could drop out.

It was Dad who changed my mind, using the simplest and most effective method—bribery. He paid me to keep going. If Mom had found out she'd have thrown a fit. Dad warned me never to let on that he was beefing up my bank account, and occasionally treating me to a cheeseburger and a strawberry milkshake on the way home, as I struggled with my brush pen and vocabulary exercises.

By then, Megan's commitment to me and the Chinese lessons had faded. She auditioned for the Drama Club musical and landed the part of the dumb girlfriend of a brainless guy with a leather jacket and greasy hair. She was thrilled, but I was pretty sure she got the part because of her long blond hair and pretty face. Her commitment to the musical meant that more and more often Dad and I made the trip to Toronto on our own.

By the time I had logged two years with Frank Wu, with his weak chin and caved-in chest and goofy laugh, I could carry on a conversation in Mandarin and read and write a couple of hundred characters. And, to my surprise as much as my parents', I began my third year with no whining and excuses.

I liked being able to talk in another language—really talk, about everyday things, not chant brainless phrases that weren't connected to anything, like we did in French class at school. I had to give "Flank" credit. He drilled us and forced us to talk to him and each other in Chinese.

Being able to mumble remarks that no one understood, and sometimes swear at people without their knowing, was an added benefit. Many times, I basked in the sense of superiority it gave me. I was probably the only person in Milford who could speak Mandarin.

There was one thing I didn't like, and never really got comfortable with. It came up in the second lesson. We sat in hard-backed chairs, with winter rain beating on the window, listening to Frank drone on about the writing system. My mind wandered and I looked around at the other students.

"Many Chinese characters," Frank lectured in his fluty voice as he stood at the blackboard with a piece of chalk in his hand, "have two parts, either top-and-bottom or left-and-right. In most cases these parts are words themselves. Example." He spun around and wrote three characters on the board. "Man, or male. This character means field, a piece of land. This one is strength or power. When you put field on top of strength, it forms a new word, *man*."

"Sounds like a guy made up *this* writing system," joked Elaine, a twenty-something African-Canadian.

Frank smiled when Tony, a Canadian-born Chinese, said, "It's all neat and logical. It makes sense, and it's easy to remember."

"How about the word for female?" Peggy asked. She was a recent arrival from Hong Kong. "Is it logical, too?"

Frank scratched his head. "Well, it looks like this." And he wrote a simple character on the board.

"Just like that?" I asked. "Three lines?"

"Strokes, Grace. The lines are called strokes."

Peggy giggled. "The strokes look like the gentle curves of our bodies."

"Or not," Susan hissed under her breath. She was middle-aged and a bit chubby.

I said, "Is that what the word is based on, our bodies?"

Frank flushed, probably regretting the whole idea of the lesson. "Perhaps you won't like the answer. This character came from an old ideograph of a person kneeling in subservience."

Elaine groaned. "I might have known."

"But," Frank said, "to make you feel better, let's do this."

He added a few strokes to the top of the word *female*, like a hat. "Now you get a new word, *an*, which means peace. Now, that's a good thing, isn't it?"

"Is that the same *an* as in Tiananmen Square?" Susan asked.

"Yes. *Tiananmen*—the Heaven Peace Gate or Gate of Heavenly Peace."

"Not much peace there in 1989," I said. "Nobody knows how many people were killed."

"And no apology from the government," Susan added.

"Come on, no politics," Tony complained. "You can discuss it after class."

"All I was trying to do," our teacher said, "was help you find a way of remembering the characters. There are thousands of them. Every little trick helps. Now look at this. If we put the word *son* beside the word for female, we get *hao*, which means good."

"Why is that?" I said. "Woman plus son means good? The Chinese don't like daughters? Is that why the orphanages are full of girls?"

PART FOUR

Milford, Ontario, and Shanghai

GRACE

❀

I was sixteen when I learned I was a "person of colour." Dad was watching some panel discussion on TV where half a dozen people sitting at a big round table competed to see who could be most profound. Or boring. Each one talked as if he or she had a lock on the world's supply of knowledge. Each was of "non-European descent"—a term used by the moderator, an author with a crooked nose and long frizzy hair that fell to the shoulders of his black leather vest.

"When's this over?" I asked.

"Soon. It's a pretty good discussion of identity politics."

"I'll bet," I said, sitting down. I had no intention of asking what identity politics meant. My show would start in ten minutes.

The men and women pounded each other with words. Big words. The only thing they agreed on was that society didn't treat "persons of colour" equally. My father didn't seem to realize that they were talking about me.

In Milford you could count on two hands the families of colour. Growing up a Parker, I had never thought of myself as ethnic, part of a visible minority, a hyphenated Canadian. I *knew* but I didn't *realize*, if that makes any sense.

One of my elementary-school teachers, during a history lesson that stressed multiculturalism, asked me how long my parents had lived in Canada.

"They were born here," I told him.

"And where did their parents come from?"

"Same thing," I replied, feeling the eyes of the other kids crawling on my back. The teacher began to prattle on about how much "other cultures" had contributed to Canadian life. He meant well, I guess.

By the time I was in high school, I was fed up with people who needed to label me in some way before they felt comfortable. I hated the Chinese-Canadian tag and resented being lumped in with kids like Amy Diep, whose family were Vietnamese "boat people," or Winston Song, whose mother could be found at any hour of the day behind the counter of the family's milk-store-plus-gas-station, selling ice cream bars and magazines, asking kids (like me) for I.D. before she'd sell them a pack of smokes, and contributing to the town stereotype that all Koreans owned a variety store. Once, I told Bobby McKay to piss off when he asked me to help him with his "Flags of the World" geography project. He was doing Japan.

At the same time, though, I envied the Songs, the Dieps, and the Lee family because they were all just that—families. Their parents spoke with accents. They ate their own kinds of food at dinner, and the better-off ones took trips "back home" to visit relatives, returning with lots of loot and photos of temples and gardens.

I was neither and nothing. A yellow face in a white family where freckles were the norm. Even my hair, according to a murder mystery I had watched on TV, was different, not just in colour but shape and texture. I didn't fit. I was a Parker but I wasn't. There were times when I felt like I didn't really belong to our family, mostly when I looked at photos of the four of us. Mom is fair haired, plump, and pear shaped, and she'd kill me if she heard me use that description. Dad has red hair, or used to, and freckles on his face and arms. Megan is in between, and very good looking. More obvious than my "ethnic" appearance is my height. I'm five-ten while all three would have trouble topping five-eight.

I've never had trouble because I'm not white. It's not a racial thing. I've never felt like a victim of society. Sure, I've heard "Chink" behind my back, and in grade eight one guy called me "Rice-head" a few times. But he was a loser and everybody but him knew it. The people on the show Dad was watching were, as far as I was concerned, full of shit.

My parents and sister, even when we fight, have always treated me as if I came out of my mother's womb in Milford's Soldiers' Memorial Hospital just like Megan did. I've always known I was adopted, but I always knew I was a Parker, too.

Maybe it's all connected to Mom's constant campaign to keep me in touch with my roots. I always hated that. Maybe my parents should have told me they knew nothing about my birth mother. Maybe they should have made up a story that they had picked me up at an adoption agency in Beijing or somewhere and left it at that. I wish they had.

You can't be two people at the same time—not without ending up in a mental institution. I'm not just Grace Parker. I've accepted that. I wasn't born at Soldiers' Memorial. I was unwanted by my so-called real parents. That's the hard part, like a toothache that won't go away. They got rid of me. When I was little I fantasized that there was some romantic, adventurous, tragic reason why they couldn't raise me themselves and I was torn from their loving arms as woeful music played in the background. But, seeing girls I know get pregnant and give up their babies, hearing stories on the news about mothers and fathers who beat up their kids or neglect them so badly they're taken away by Children's Aid—all that taught me that kids are sometimes not wanted, or even hated. Some parents would gladly get rid of their kid if they could. Mine had.

Low self-esteem is my problem, according to my guidance counsellor in grade ten. She seemed to think that by hanging a label on the issue she had solved it. We had quite a few sessions for a while when I was failing tests and skipping classes and mouthing off at my teachers. I have low self-esteem, she said, so I was "acting out." She had to go to university and get a degree to discover that? I thought I was just being a bitch. How high would her self-esteem be, I wanted to ask, if she knew her mother didn't want her and had got rid of her after she was born?

It's something I've never been able to shake. All the good will and kind words can't change anything, so they just make me angry. I sometimes wonder if I wasn't Asian, would I still have this feeling of not belonging, this sense that everybody is only *pretending* I'm a Parker? My hair, skin, and eyes are banners flagging my status as a drop-in visitor. I'm supposed to be proud I'm Chinese, like Mom says? Glad to be a person of colour?

I don't remember when I began to fantasize about going to China. Would that help? Maybe, I'd think sometimes. Probably not, I'd tell myself at other times. But I couldn't stop seeing my life as a jigsaw puzzle with one piece missing. I often imagined myself tracking down the two people who left me on the steps of the orphanage, knocking on their door.

"Thanks for the baggage," I'd say.

I tried to sound calm but my heart raced up to my throat and I almost choked on a mouthful of apple pie. "I think I've decided what I'd like for my graduation present."

I paused for a few seconds, waiting for my parents to pay attention.

"And my birthday is six months away, so this will be a two-in-one deal."

"Good," my father joked. "I'll save a bundle."

My eyes met Megan's. She looked a bit uneasy, but gave me a thumbs-up that my parents didn't see. "You know what Mom and Dad are like," she had reminded me three times that week. "They always ask us way ahead of time what gift we'd like for an occasion. Your graduation is coming up, so you need to let them know our plan. They have to be prepared. We can't drop it on them like a nuclear bomb."

"You might be surprised," I told Dad, pausing again, hoping to build the suspense. Megan isn't the only dramatic daughter in this family, I thought.

My mother merely nodded, avoiding my eyes. Dad gazed at me expectantly. The whistling kettle brought Megan to her feet. She rushed into the kitchen, which was completely unlike her.

"Now I *am* curious," Dad said.

"Wait 'til Meagan comes back," I said.

"Tea is ready, ladies and gentleman," Megan announced cheerfully. Holding the blue and white teapot in her mittened palms, she looked like the most awkward waitress in the world. "Did you tell them?" she asked.

"No, I waited for you. You're in on this, too."

"Come on, Grace, what's the big surprise?" Mom asked.

I pulled a pamphlet out of my back pocket and held it up in front of me like a prize. "Huang-pu Summer Institute" it said in bold, flowing letters across a photo showing a river in the foreground and a cityscape in the background. "Shanghai, China, 1999." I put the pamphlet down in front of my plate.

My parents looked at it as if a crow had just flown over and left a deposit.

"For my combined birthday/graduation present I would like an airline ticket to China," I announced.

You'd have thought I had said "I'm pregnant" or "I'm running away with a fifty-five-year-old plumber." Silence fell like a bag of wet sand. Mom poked a bit of pie crust around on her plate with her fork. Dad swallowed and looked at my mother, waiting for her reaction.

I wondered if she was surprised. After all, it was she who had pushed me all my life to get to know China, to learn Chinese, to continue with private lessons to this day. And it was Mom, not Dad, who had insisted that she was Number Two Mama and Chun-mei was Number One.

Mother finally said something. "It's a big step, Grace, going to school in another country. On your own."

"Mom, it's a great opportunity. Frank told me all about it and gave me the application forms last week. Huang-pu Business College runs an intensive Mandarin course for three weeks. Frank says I can easily qualify for the intermediate level. It's part of their international business program. And since I want to do business studies at university, it's perfect. The China-Canada Co-operation Society is promoting it. They also have a graduate program at Huang-pu. So if I like it there, I can—"

"Whoa, slow down!" Dad said, picking up the pamphlet and opening it.

"And the best part," Megan put in, "is that there's a two-week guided cultural tour of five cities in China when the course is finished. Can I tell them, Grace?"

I nodded.

"Here's the second part of the news. Cheers, everybody," Megan gushed, holding up her teacup. "I'm going to join Grace for the cultural tour."

My parents looked at each other, exactly as they had when I was nine and my sister and I had brought a stray cat home to the house, announcing that we had adopted her.

"Hey, all of you," Megan put in, "take it easy, will you? It's about time you saw your investment pay off—the Chinese lessons for me and Grace, the gas consumed to take us there week after week, not to mention our putting up with Frank, listening to his endless stories—well, in my case, until I quit." She raised her teacup again. "Everyone, *gan-bei!* Cheers!"

My father followed her lead. "I think it's a great idea," he said.

My mother said nothing.

That night, Mom came into my room, closed the door behind her, and sat on the edge of my bed. I was sitting up against the headboard, reading a travel book on China.

Mom gathered her housecoat tighter at the throat. She looked tense and sad at the same time. "When you go there," she began, "are you planning to look for Chun-mei?"

I lowered my book. I'd thought about this a lot. "I don't know, Mom. One minute I want to, another I don't. Maybe I'll chicken out and just be a tourist."

She nodded without saying anything.

"Mom, when I was growing up, you and Dad, particularly you, always made a big thing about my Chinese roots, and the so-called Number One Mama. I hated you for it then, you know. I didn't want two mothers. Now I think I understand what you were trying to do."

Mom began to cry quietly. "I wanted you to know about your birth mother because it's the right thing to do. But now that maybe you'll meet her, I feel jealous. I don't want to share you with anyone."

She leaned close and I put my arms around her. "Mom," I said. "You're my mother and this is my family. China is where I came from. This is what I am."

JANE

(1999)

Oh, wasn't I the open-minded one! Insisting that Dong-mei stay connected to her roots, even calling myself "Mama Number Two," until doing so upset her so much I backed off. Taking her to Chinatown, pushing her to take Chinese lessons. Wasn't I the great liberal, unselfish and tolerant! Easy to do when the possibility of her ever wanting to find her birth mother was so remote, never mind actually tracking Chun-mei down. Now I feel like a hypocrite and a fool.

Kevin was skeptical from the start, but he went along with me, the teacher who knew all about children, who had taken all those psychology courses at university, the woman who, as it turned out, didn't know a damn thing. It was all theory, all talk. My daughter had had no interest in China or her original family. Why should she? All she knew was Kevin and me and Megan, our house in Milford, her school, her friends. What did she care about a country far away, even if she was born there?

But no one could tell me that. I had to insist, had to push. As she matured into a young woman, I hardly noticed her gradual change in attitude, her growing interest in China. Kevin had always wanted Dong-mei to take a business degree at university, and once I overheard him talking about what a great asset her knowledge of the Chinese language would be in the future. She didn't fly into a rage the way she would have when she was a child. But none of that sank in.

When she made her birthday request at the dinner table, it struck me like a punch in the stomach. I could hardly speak. No, I wanted to say to her, you can't go! You're *my* daughter. *I* raised you. Insanely, I thought about my lost baby. I recalled the time I walked Megan to kindergarten on her first day of school, then years later took the same route with Dong-mei. I relived the aching sense of loss that only a mother can understand.

Of course Dong-mei has a right to know, to search out her birth parents, find closure—a word I hate. She's entitled to have a relationship with them if she wants to. It's up to her. I know all that. Haven't I said it enough times? But it's different when it happens to you. I don't want to share her with a stranger. She's ours.

GRACE

(1999)

Dawn broke in unmoving air, threatening yet another hot and sticky day. As I helped Dad load my luggage into the van after breakfast, our street was already filled with the tuneless buzz of air conditioners.

I said goodbye to Megan in the driveway. She stood in her pyjamas and slippers, hair in a tangle, half asleep. "See you in a few weeks," she said. She'd be joining me after my classes for the cultural tour.

I half expected to see Frank when we walked into the departure terminal, even though we had said our goodbyes the night before. He had left our house near midnight after going through my travel plans with me for the third time. Inside my backpack was a piece of paper listing four contacts in China that he had set up for me. Dad had made two extra copies, one in each suitcase, "just in case." In the past few weeks, Frank and I had spent hours bent over the map of China spread across our dining-room table. He had come up with a plan.

Ms. Song, a classmate of Frank's from his university years, would meet me at the airport.

"Don't worry," he repeated endlessly. "She knows who you are."

He had sent Song my graduation photo. A little anxious about getting lost in an airport in a strange city, I was grateful for Frank's help, but I had always known that with him everything was complicated.

"If Ms. Song isn't there when you arrive," Frank urged, "don't wait for her. Take a taxi to the Dragon Gate Hotel downtown. Your room is booked."

I would be staying there for a few days until the college dorms were available.

"But I should wait for her. What if she gets caught in traffic? She'll arrive expecting to find me and I'll be gone."

"No, no, that's not in the plan. Go to the hotel right away. If she doesn't show up by eleven o'clock the next morning, phone Mr. Kang, the second name on the list."

"Shouldn't I call Ms. Song first? It would be rude to ignore—"

"No, you can't. Song didn't give me her phone number. Kang gave me his."

Mr. Kang was the brother-in-law of Frank's cousin.

My stomach leapt when Dad said, "Well, Grace, I think it's time." Mom, who had been silent since we had pulled out of our driveway, seemed to wake from a dream.

"Now, remember, Grace, you're to call us every Saturday night."

"Yes, Mom."

"That's Sunday morning our time."

"Yes, Mom."

"Frank says you can buy long-distance cards in China."

"Yes, Mom."

"If not, call collect."

"Mom, we've been through this."

She pointed with her chin towards the security gate and gave me a tearful smile. "The longest journey begins with the first step," she said with a lame attempt at light-heartedness. It was an old Chinese proverb.

I hugged my parents, feeling an unexpected lump in my throat and a sudden twinge of anxiety. If the flight had been cancelled at that moment I would have sighed with relief and gone home.

Through the window of the departure lounge I watched airplanes come and go. I thought about a classical Chinese novel, *Journey to the West*, a four-volume set in English that my parents had bought for my birthday. I laughed at the cover, which showed a shabbily dressed priest on a horse, accompanied by a monkey, a guy with a pig's face, and a bearded friar, all on foot. And I don't mean the guy had a face *like* a pig; it *was* a pig face. This is a five-hundred-year-old classic? I had thought. I had plowed through all four volumes, though, skimming along and skipping over bits. The book is about a quest to find the place where a sacred Buddhist book is located. Although there were no guns or explosions, I half expected Indiana Jones to pop up at any moment.

I wasn't looking for hidden treasure or sacred writings. All I wanted were a few answers, and the older I got, the stronger was my desire to know. Whatever happened, at least I'd be able to tell myself, and my kids if I had any, that I had tried.

Frank had a boyhood friend in Yangzhou named Xu who had recently been laid off by the textile factory where he had worked for more than twenty years. Xu may have been unlucky in his job but he was a terrific detective. He had hunted down Mrs. Xia, the woman from the orphanage whom my parents had met. She was retired, in her seventies, Xu had written. He had also said Miss Canada—me—had better come soon before Xia was "summoned by the clouds." I had her address among the other contacts Frank had provided.

I had read lots of articles about ordinary people—as well as celebrities—who had reunited with their birth parents. The reunions seemed to make them all famous. I had no illusions about a Disney-style ending for myself, though. I wanted to see Chun-mei's face, and her husband's too. If she refused to answer my questions, I would walk away.

Journey to the West, I said to myself as my plane taxied down the runway. I would be entering China from their east. But I would be referred to as a Westerner. Although there were no mountains of knives for me to climb, as described in the novel, no burning sea to sail across, knowing that didn't make me feel any better.

The roller-coaster landing at Hongqiao Airport in Shanghai left me nauseated even after I had cleared the passport check and collected my luggage, so when I heard a voice asking in Mandarin, "Are you Grace? From Canada?" it didn't register at first. I stopped, and the rushing stream of travellers flowed around me as people hurried for the exits, calling out and getting in each other's way.

"Grace?"

A small middle-aged woman smiled as she opened a wallet and held it up. The scene reminded me of the old spy movies my dad loved so much. Inside the clear plastic pocket a fresh-faced girl in a borrowed gown smiled at me. It was my graduation photo.

"Yes, that's me."

Hot and sweaty, no doubt smelly, in a crumpled shirt and shorts, I didn't remotely resemble the girl in the picture. I had been on the road for more than twenty-four hours by then, and I was jet-lagged and exhausted.

Ms. Song tried to wave off a cluster of porters who offered to carry my luggage even though I had already piled it on a cart.

"Two U.S. dollar," one said, holding up two fingers and grabbing at my backpack with his other hand.

"One dollar only!" another shouted.

"*Gun-kai!*" Song said brusquely. "Go away! We don't need you."

"We are not talking to you, woman," the younger one snapped. "She's rich. What do you care if we make a little money?"

"*Xiang-xia-ren!*" Song shot back, leading me and my cart through the crowd.

Xiang-xia-ren meant country folk, I knew from my Mandarin lessons, but it obviously suggested more than that, judging from the men's reaction and the way Song spat out the words.

Outside, the air was sticky and oppressive. Song hailed a taxi and chatted away to the driver in Shanghai dialect, which I couldn't follow. It was near midnight by the time I checked into the Dragon Gate Hotel. Although my body felt like a limp rope, my mind was racing with excitement, and I knew I wouldn't sleep for a while. Song went to a table near the window and made tea from a large thermos.

"Guess how old I am," she asked shortly after we settled into the two large armchairs.

"Um, I don't know. It's hard to say. It's sort of dark in here. Thirty?"

She laughed. "Be serious."

"Thirty-five?"

Song was barely five feet tall, with a slight build. Her straight black hair was cut short at her earlobes. Behind her square-framed glasses her face was unwrinkled. But Frank had told me they had been classmates at university, so I knew she must be older.

"Forty-five!" she crowed. "I'm old enough to be your mother, although my own daughter is only fifteen. How old is your mother? Is she a blonde?"

"She'd kill me if I told her age. She's older than you. She used to be blond, like my sister Megan, and both have blue eyes. But Mom's hair is salt-and-pepper now, more salt."

"Salt-and-pepper! What a vivid description. In China we have only three hair colours—black, grey, and white. Very boring."

"I guess that's what's in store for me," I said.

"But you have choices. I heard that in your country people dye their hair any colour they want. Even orange or green. And in a movie I saw that you identify one another by hair and eye colour. It's so strange."

We chatted for a while about clothing, make-up, and other stuff that Song was interested in. She wanted to know if it was true that all Western women were overweight.

"I'm not," I said.

"But you're Chinese!"

I laughed. I knew we'd get along fine.

I said goodbye to Song before she got into her taxi, and watched the tail lights move out of sight, then walked back up the steps to the hotel. At the top, I turned towards the din of traffic and human voices at the Shanghai train station, with its bright red neon tower. The wide space before the front doors was packed with people, standing, sitting, laid out on thin rush mats—thousands of people in the middle of the night, caught between home and somewhere else.

I would have slept the whole day through if Ms. Song hadn't knocked on my door. My watch said five past five in the afternoon, and I thought instantly about the argument I'd had with my parents, telling them I was too young to suffer from jet lag. I pulled on my clothes, ran a comb through my hair, and let Song in. She drew open the curtains to reveal a hazy sky.

"I've come to take you sight-seeing!"

Though still half-asleep, I did some mental calculations. Song had been up half the night taking care of me and then had put in a full day's work. "I don't want to put you to any trouble, Ms. Song," I said.

"Call me Julia. I may not be able to visit you tomorrow or the next day. I have a crazy schedule at the office."

"Julia?" I hesitated.

"I've been called Julia for two years now. At work. Choosing an English name is part of the package. I used to teach English at a textile college in the suburbs. After eighteen years, I quit. I'd finally had enough, the unfair treatment from my colleagues and leaders at the college. Now I work for Eastern Wing Airlines, a Hong Kong company with a busy branch here. I'm a ticket agent."

"You quit college teaching to be a ticket agent?" I said tactlessly. Song's openness was infectious.

"Believe it or not, I make more money now than I used to, with a bonus at the end of the year if the boss is happy with the profits. That never happened at the college. I got this job because I could read and speak English. If I didn't have English, the boss would have tossed my application out the window without blinking an eye."

Remembering my manners, I set about making two cups of tea.

"In today's market," Song said, "women my age, anyone over forty, are unemployable. Those who work in state-owned factories are forced to retire, to make room for younger ones who need jobs. But of course the new policy doesn't apply to men."

"I wish my mother were here to hear this," I put in. "In Canada a company with this kind of policy would be in deep trouble for sex discrimination. And age discrimination."

"Ha! Go tell that to my turkey-neck boss. He is over seventy but he demands that all the women he hires be twenty-five or less, with fair skin and fine features."

"You mean a pretty face is what they want."

"Yes. I feel lucky, compared to most women my age."

I still wasn't clear why selling airline tickets was better than teaching at a university. "So what's this about getting the cold treatment you mentioned earlier?" I asked.

"It's a bit complicated," she said, taking a sip of her tea. "Your family friend, Frank, and I are what we call WPS—Worker-Peasant-Soldier university graduates. We went to university during the Cultural Revolution, which lasted from 1966 to 1976. Workers, peasants, and soldiers then were considered the most politically pure people in the country, while intellectuals, businesspeople, and so on were persecuted. During those years, entrance exams were abolished because they were condemned as favourable only to the non-working classes. People like me and Frank, who didn't complete high school because we were forced to work in factories or on farms, could apply for university with no exam, as long as our political record was clean.

"We were the last wave of WPS students before Deng Xiao-ping brought entrance exams back. So our time at university, particularly in our last year, was not happy, because all the students who came in after us criticized and mocked us. We were not 'real academics.' The WPS label followed us after we graduated and were assigned to jobs. Like the 'children of concubines,' we were discriminated against all through our careers."

"Interesting expression," I said, "the children of concubines."

"Yes. It's from the old pre-liberation days, when the

emperors and high officials were entitled to have one wife but as many concubines as they pleased. The children of their wives were much higher in status than the kids the concubines produced. Anyhow, no matter what I did in my new teaching job, I couldn't wipe out the past. I took extra courses on weekends and in the evenings. I postponed marriage and starting a family. My daughter was born when I was thirty. Still, nothing satisfied my boss or the university administration, and I got no respect from my co-workers or students. I was given all the worst classes and the junior students. No promotion, no research assignments. I wasn't ashamed of being WPS and I made that clear, which didn't help me. So finally, I left. And as you know, Frank went abroad. But enough lecturing! I sound like a teacher again."

The Green Villa restaurant was on Nanjing Road, which must be the most crowded street in the world. Most of the tables were occupied. We were shown upstairs to a table by the window. I sat down, grateful for the air conditioning, and Song began to chat with the waiter. He went away and returned to hand me a menu in English.

I put it aside. "I don't need this, but thanks anyway," I said.

"I know you don't need it," Song replied, "but it will help me. I don't have enough English to describe the fancy food and cooking here. I'm hoping you'll explain a few things to me."

Next to us a party was in progress, with six adults and a boy of about five or six. The obnoxious little creep was anywhere but in his chair. He spent his time crawling among the other tables and roaming around the dining room, annoying other diners, all the while chased by a young woman with a bowl of rice in one hand and a spoon in the other, trying to feed the brat as he scooted from place to place.

I thought about my dad and his motto: if a kid doesn't eat, he isn't hungry. I had often argued with him about that, wanting to play and eat at the same time, or eat in front of the TV. Dad would have ended this little troublemaker's travels fast. I told Song that the kid reminded me of the spoiled boy-king in the movie *The Last Emperor*.

"Yes, boys like him *are* called little emperors nowadays," she answered in English. "Look at him, doted on by everyone. I bet his poor mother hasn't had a bite yet, but the ruler of the family must not be disciplined! All because he's the only child—and a boy."

"And the girls are empresses?"

"Oh, no. I'm afraid China still has feudal attitudes about this matter, especially in the countryside, where boys are preferred. Surprised?"

"Well . . ."

"Don't worry, it doesn't mean that all girl children are mistreated or undervalued. Look, I have a daughter and I wouldn't trade her for a dozen sons. Nor would my husband."

"But don't more than eighty percent of Chinese live in the country? What's the problem there that they're still so behind the times? They're educated, right? They have radios, and TV?"

"I'm sorry I upset you, Grace," Song said quietly.

"No, no, it wasn't you," I said. "I was thinking out loud."

At that moment the little boy scooted under our table

for the third time. I had to force myself not to boot him in his fat little ass.

I spent the next morning killing time by exploring the Bund and waterfront area. It wasn't very interesting. On the way back to the hotel I walked through a shopping district on Nanjing Road. Almost all the store windows were jammed with high-fashion, logo-covered clothing, cosmetics and perfume, or high-tech computer and entertainment equipment. A giant picture of the latest Western supermodel, with long blond hair and a body as thin as a coat hanger, advertised Rolex watches across the road from a fast-food stall where workers in faded denim pants and threadbare T-shirts lined up to buy fried bread. So much for the socialist workers' paradise.

My room was cool. I kicked off my shoes and lay on the bed and fell asleep instantly. I awoke to a knocking on the door. Song was standing there with a young girl.

"Say hello, *Ah-yi*," Song told the girl, who mumbled something. *Ah-yi*—Auntie—was a term of respect. "Speak louder, she can't hear you. This is my daughter, Xing-xing. She has never been inside a fancy hotel like this. I hope you don't mind that I brought her."

"No, of course not," I said. "Come on in."

I made tea for Song and myself and offered a cola to Xing-xing. Like her mother, Xing-xing had almond-shaped eyes, which gave her a fragile appearance. She would have been prettier without the blue eyeshadow, vivid red lipstick, and a thick layer of blush on her cheeks. Her long black hair was piled on her head and decorated with a red ribbon that contrasted with her tight green T-shirt. She was wearing a denim miniskirt and fishnet stockings. She looked like a wannabe hooker in a second-rate movie.

"Tell *Ah-yi* what you want to be when you grow up," Song said to Xing-xing after we had sat down.

"You tell her, Mama."

Song turned pink, and I smothered a laugh.

"Don't be ridiculous, you useless girl. Look at *Ah-yi*. She is a Chinese like you, only four years older, yet she speaks English, French, and Chinese. She is going to university to get a good education. She'll have a wonderful job and make a lot of money. Don't you want the same things? Speak up!" Song demanded when her daughter said nothing.

"Why do you want Xing-xing to be like me?" I asked in English. "You hardly know me. And who told you I am rich? I'm just an ordinary person, Julia."

"But you have a wonderful life in Canada," she replied in Mandarin. "Don't be so modest. Most Chinese girls would die to have what you have."

To change the subject, I suggested we go to the hotel restaurant for dinner. Song happily agreed. When the three of us had sat down at a table in the busy dining room and ordered our food, Xing-xing began to play with the glass lazy susan in the centre of the table. Song talked to me in English.

"I want to ask if you can help Xing-xing to go to a Canadian university when the time comes."

"Um, well, I could try," I said lamely. "Are you planning to move to Canada?"

Song laughed. "Oh, no. That would be impossible. But I will send Xing-xing abroad if I can."

"But she'd be away for a year at a time. Wouldn't you and your husband miss her?"

"Of course we would. But it's a sacrifice we would gladly make for Xing-xing's future. You'll understand when you become a mother yourself."

"Speaking of school," I said, "the residence at Huang-pu College opens tomorrow."

"Yes, a pity you must move from this nice hotel," Song said.

The Huang-pu Business College was in the old French section of Shanghai, on a wide street lined with plane trees and free of the constant snarl of traffic that seemed to clog most of the city. The school was housed in an old mansion with a large courtyard and a new wing added to the back—the dorms, I learned soon after my arrival.

Classes were held in the original mansion, in grand rooms with hardwood floors, high ceilings, and large windows looking out over the courtyard. There were two dozen of us in the summer institute, people about my age from Canada, the United States and Europe. I was not used to the teaching style. Where Frank had an iron rule that, when he and I were together, not one word of English was to be spoken, our Chinese teacher lectured, giving us no chance to talk to her in Mandarin. That was for the language lab, she told us on the first day. Her job was to teach us grammar.

Besides the lab and lectures each day, we had calligraphy lessons that were more like an art class, taught by a skinny old guy named Lao Qin who stood over us chattering away and pointing out faults in our brush strokes. But it was the only class I enjoyed—not just because he favoured me, being the only "overseas Chinese" in the class, but because I liked the feel of the brush in my hand and the way the jet-black ink flowed from the brush onto the newspaper we used for practice.

At night, most of the other students went out drinking at the disco bars. I went with them once. The bars were incredibly hot, pounding with tenth-rate rock music, and every once in a while they'd fire up the karaoke machine. There were hookers there, and drugs. So much for Mom's notion that China was free of vice. We got back to the school at three in the morning, wasted and red-eyed. Once was enough for me.

In the middle of the third week, Dad called. He told me that Megan had come down with a bad case of appendicitis and had had an operation. "Don't worry," he said to calm me, "it was a simple procedure and she sailed through it. She's home now, doing fine and grumping at everybody. But she won't be able to join your tour group."

The longer I was in China, the more I felt my birth parents pulling me towards them, as if a big question was closer to an answer if only I'd take a few more steps. I wasn't far away. But I was afraid of what I might find out. By the last week of classes I still hadn't made up my mind. Then one morning I stood at the sink and looked at the face in the mirror, the black hair, the dark skin, the large eyes that were not reflected in my sister or my parents. I decided what I wanted to do.

I passed all my courses and so did everybody else. At the little graduation tea party out on the lawn under the plane trees, everyone was abuzz about the five-city tour—Suzhou, Hangzhou, and Wuxi, which were not too far from Shanghai, then Beijing and Xi'an.

I told the director of the summer institute that I'd be visiting relatives instead of taking the tour. "No refund," was his answer.

"I don't care," I said. "I've got other plans."

After the party, I went to my dorm and called Song to say goodbye and to tell her I was going to Yangzhou. She insisted on getting my train ticket for me.

"There is no train to Yangzhou," she said. "You have to take a train to Zhenjiang and then catch a bus. It's very difficult for you to get a train ticket, but for me it's as easy as cutting a piece of bean curd. My work unit and the train station are co-ordinated units, as we call it. We do favours for one another all the time. What do you say in English? We back-scratch each other."

I laughed. "Something like that. Okay, I'll go ahead and book a hotel room in Yangzhou."

"There's no need to book ahead," Song said, "so save yourself the cost of a long-distance call. Look, this is Shanghai, and your hotel wasn't full when you arrived, so Yangzhou will have lots of empty rooms. If you call ahead for a reservation, you will be charged full price. But if you just walk into the hotel in Yangzhou and ask if there's a room, you can get a bargain. I wish you would stay in Shanghai a few days longer," she went on. "My husband and I would like you to visit our home."

"That's very kind of you," I said. "But I have a tight schedule. My visa is only good for two more weeks and I don't know what kind of problems or delays I might run into."

"Then wait for my call tomorrow morning. I'll have your ticket, possibly see you off at the station."

By the time I boarded the train for Zhenjiang and took a window seat in the air-conditioned car, my mood was lighter and I felt kind of proud of myself. I had accomplished a lot in the past two days.

The high point in my morning had been my visit to the ticket office in the train station. Carrying my backpack and clutching my suitcase, I had felt like royalty as I walked past the long queues—or rather crowds—gathered in an unruly bunch in front of the ticket windows, greeted by hostile stares and grumbling. I had stepped into a room where I presented my confirmation number, provided by Song, paid for my ticket, and left. The whole procedure took less than fifteen minutes. The man behind the wicket even apologized to me because there were no first-class tickets left.

Hours later, the train made its slow progress out of Shanghai station. Only at that moment did I feel that my journey was finally under way.

As the train arrived at Zhenjiang station, I got my first glimpse of Frank's hometown. It seemed to be a city of chimneys, all pumping clouds of black smoke into the hot, sticky air. The walls of the buildings were the colour of ashes. Not much concern for greenhouse emissions here, I thought as I got down from the train amid the clanging of the bell and the rumble of the bustling crowd.

As soon as I emerged from the station into the square I was swarmed by four women who plucked at my sleeves and the back my shirt, demanding something. Each of them had a long-handled cotton bag hanging around her neck and each strove to shout louder than the others.

A small crowd quickly gathered to watch the show as the two loudest women attempted to drag me in opposite directions.

"What the hell are you doing?" I yelled back in Mandarin, startled by the assault. "Let go of me!"

They switched from local dialect to Mandarin after they heard me yell, and I soon realized that they were looking for customers for the taxis waiting nearby. The tallest one snatched my suitcase from my hand, hooked her arm in mine, and pulled me towards a white minibus whose engine rattled as if it would die at any minute.

Her competitors had gone off to attack other prey. Inside the minibus, a few passengers, sweating and wrinkled, sat watching the driver yell at an old man behind him.

"No money, no ride! I am not running a buddha temple! Get off the bus!"

The old man hawked loudly and spat out the window before he climbed out slowly. He spat again, this time onto the floor of the vehicle, then shuffled away.

"Where you go, young miss?" the woman asked me again, pushing her hair back from her sweaty brow.

I explained that I wanted to go to the central station to catch a bus to Yangzhou.

"No need," she said. "We can take you to Yangzhou, direct and cheap. Ten yuan."

"Okay."

I got in and took the old man's place, wrinkling my nose

at his gamey odour. The woman shoved my suitcase beside me and took her seat next to the driver, who rammed the gear shift forward and moved off.

She turned and asked, "Where in Yangzhou?" She sounded friendly now.

"Yangzhou Hotel," I said.

The minibus pitched and jumped along the road, the engine protesting, the air inside oppressively hot. Each time I opened the window, clouds of choking dust and more hot air swept in. When we arrived at the station, an hour and a half later, two of the passengers got out.

"Stay on," the woman said to me. There was a quick exchange between her and the driver before the bus was under way again. "We will drop you off at the hotel. It's on our way."

In my room, I made myself a cup of tea. The hotel, like the one in Shanghai, provided a large thermos of boiled water, cups, and a few packets of jasmine tea. I stood at the window, enjoying the relatively cool air, looking down into the street and watching the blazing sun sink behind a cluster of two-storey buildings. I was a step closer to my goal. I had a room in the city that my parents had not been allowed to visit, where Chun-mei had abandoned me. Right this moment, I realized with a shiver, I could take a taxi to the orphanage and walk up those same steps.

Instead, I locked my door, stripped off my clothes, turned on the shower and stood under it for a long time. I put on loose-fitting pants and a fresh T-shirt and combed my hair back with my fingers. With a fresh cup of tea before me, I sat at the desk and thumbed through my tour book.

Yangzhou had been an imperial retreat for the court of the Qing dynasty more than a hundred years before, with pavilions hung with famous paintings, performances by storytellers and opera stars, libraries filled with the works of renowned scholars. But nothing of that remained. What the Taiping Rebels hadn't destroyed in the early nineteenth century, the Red Guards burned and smashed in the twentieth. The ruins of the old town in the northwest part of Yangzhou were all that was left.

Checking a local map I had picked up at the front desk, I found Mrs. Xia's street. I intended to visit her first thing in the morning.

After a hasty breakfast of toast and tea—the waitress gave me a curious look when I turned down the delights of rice gruel, pickled vegetables, deep-fried dough sticks, and boiled eggs—I threw a couple of bottles of water and my guide book into my backpack and took the stairs down to the lobby.

The old man who had given me a good room at a good price the day before because I had "come home from across the sea" was behind the desk, reading a newspaper spread out before him. His bald spot, encircled by a monkish fringe of grey hair, reflected the overhead light.

I asked him the quickest way to the ruins. I was confident that, once in that area, I could easily find my way to my true destination. He spread out my map on top of the newspaper. "It's two blocks from Guanyin Hill," he said cheerfully. "The ruin is all we have left. It's a miracle it survived. But there are still a few statues standing." He looked up at me over his glasses. "Do they have Guanyin where you come from? The Goddess of Mercy? She's really hot these days. Worshipped by everyone. Go see her. She's the one with a baby boy in her arms. That's why she is so popular, you see. That's why so many young women pray to her."

He gave me an exaggerated wink and then drew a route on the map with his fingernail.

The area near the ruins provided the most peaceful streets I had experienced since stepping onto Chinese soil. And the sky was actually blue, unlike Shanghai and Zhenjiang. I walked along the canal that I had spotted from my hotel window. The caramel-coloured water stank of sewage and rotting vegetation. The banks were lined with single-storey houses roofed with grey tiles and separated by narrow alleys. Barges poled by skinny, bare-chested men moved up and down the canal, sending geese and ducks scurrying.

I thought about the story that I had been told and retold as a kid. Mrs. Xia was a heroine in my parents' eyes.

"She's normal height, but short," my mother had described her, typically unclear. "She's not big, even by Chinese standards," Dad had added. Both of them had agreed that Mrs. Xia must have been in her late forties or early fifties when they met her. She had come back to their hotel under the cover of darkness, clutching the piece of paper with my name and Chun-mei's on it. At this point in the story one of my parents would speculate on the risks that Xia took, the conspiratorial look in her eye as she left the hotel room.

But I had never seen it as kindness. To me, she had delivered not a piece of paper but a curse. How much simpler my life would have been without that note and the four characters written on it. I had wished that Xia had minded her own business.

I turned away from the canal. The *hu-tongs*, or alleys, twisted and curved, lined with houses whose plank doors were set back only a couple of feet from the cobblestones. The street was quiet and empty. It was siesta time, I guessed. According to Frank, the afternoon nap was an "unshakable unwritten bylaw in China." He even joked that if you woke an official from his or her nap you would guarantee failure in your mission. As I walked, my cork sandals flip-flopping on the cobblestones, I tried to calm myself, but my stomach twisted itself into a knot. What if Mrs. Xia knew nothing more than what she had passed on to my parents so long ago? Would she refuse to help me? Was she too old or sick to remember anything?

I soon lost my way in a tangle of alleys with names like Duck Feet, Swallow's Tongue, and Silver Ears. If I walk far enough, I thought, will I reach stomachs or intestines? Three times I found myself back at the canal, hot and frustrated, my map clutched uselessly in my hand. It had looked so easy back at the hotel, with the crisp new map spread out before me. At random I picked another narrow street that led back into the maze of animal-part *hu-tongs*. Then I saw the blue and white sign mounted on the grey brick of a building at an intersection. *Yu-chun-xiang*—Fish Lip Lane, Mrs. Xia's street.

I stopped in front of No. 34 and took a deep breath. Out-of-date red posters plastered on the double door offered Happy New Year greetings. I looked around one more time, then knocked. The door squeaked open a couple of inches on its own.

I could see a cramped, dimly lit room with a square table and a few benches in one corner. Closer to the door stood two rattan chairs. A plastic bead curtain with a fish design hung in the doorway leading to the back of the house. A figure appeared, holding aside the strands of the curtain, squinting into the bar of sunlight that fell through the door where I stood. She was a small, elderly woman, and with her free hand she tucked her short silver hair behind her ears. I pushed the door open further.

In a quiet, sleepy voice she said something that I couldn't make out. Meanwhile, she looked me over. I guess my foreign-looking outfit had taken her by surprise. She spoke again, louder this time but in local dialect. I shook my head.

"Mrs. Xia?" I whispered, though I wasn't sure why I kept my voice low. "Are you Mrs. Xia?"

"*Nin-shuo-shen-ma?*" she replied in heavily accented Mandarin this time, her hand cupped behind one ear. "What did you say? My ears are giving up on me."

I felt like an idiot. The problem wasn't the old lady's hearing. I had spoken in English.

"I'm sorry, Old Comrade," I answered in Chinese, feeling sillier at using such an outdated term. My nerves had taken over my brain. "I am looking for Xia . . . Xia . . ." I fumbled, searching hard for the right word.

I wasn't sure how to address Mrs. Xia properly. It was a cultural problem. In formal Chinese, "Mrs." translated as *Fu-ren,* man's person, a respectful title, although I found it pretty offensive. Or *Tai-tai,* which means wife, but it was an old-fashioned term. I didn't know if Mrs. Xia was married, so *Tai-tai* was out of the question.

"I am trying to find Xia Mama," I said.

"My name is Xia," she answered. "I am the only Xia in Fish Lip Lane, but I can't imagine I'm the one you're looking for."

I was as certain as the hard cobblestones under my feet that I was looking at the woman who had altered the course of my life soon after I was born. She began to fidget. When she touched her collar I noticed the swollen knuckles, the rough skin.

"You are . . . ," she said, walking towards me.

"Xia Mama," my lips began to tremble, "my name is Dong-mei. I am from Canada." I repeated *Jia-na-da* when she failed to react.

"I don't know anyone from Canada," she replied. "You say your name is Dong—" Her eyes searched my face. "My dear heaven," she murmured, her hand covering her mouth. "Is it possible? How could—?"

She reached out and brushed my cheek with her rough fingertips. "It's you," she whispered. "The Tearless Girl. My old eyes are not cheating me. Oh, look at me, letting a guest stand in the doorway." She threw open the door, allowing sunlight to flood into the room. "Come in and sit down, Dong-mei. You must be thirsty."

She pointed to the rattan chairs, then the bead curtain rattled and clicked as she slipped through. I heard water poured and the *poof* of a propane flame coming to life. Sitting by myself in the tiny room, I wished there was a phone handy so I could call home and share my news.

A few minutes later, Mrs. Xia appeared with a tray bearing a small earthenware teapot, two cups, a glass, and a bottle of orange pop.

"You probably prefer pop to tea," she said. "It's very hot today."

I would have preferred tea to the sugary orange water that was so popular in China. Instead I poured half the bottle into the glass and handed it to Mrs. Xia.

"Oh, no." She waved the glass away. "That stuff makes my teeth ache. The ones I have left."

We both laughed, more than her joke deserved.

In the small house in Fish Lip Lane, words flowed and ebbed all afternoon, pausing only when Mrs. Xia went into the kitchen to replenish the teapot. I struggled with my Chinese, hunting my mental vocabulary lists for the words I wanted. At one point Mrs. Xia reached over and took my hands in hers, kneading my fingers one by one. Her skin felt like sandpaper.

"This is what I did each time after I changed your diaper," she said. "I don't know where I got this peculiar habit, but it became a comfort to me, and if I didn't do it, I felt that things were not right."

"Your hands seem, well, tired," I observed.

"Oh, that," she said. "That's old age showing itself. Doctor says I have arthritis. My daughter blames it on washing bedding and clothes and diapers in cold water every day for twenty years."

"You washed everything by hand?"

"Of course. We didn't have a machine until after you went away. It was bought with your parents' donation. People said that it was so generous that we could buy all the washing machines in the People's Department Store downtown! What a godsend! We had a meeting to learn the dos and don'ts of running the machine. Also in the meeting we decided to use it to wash only heavy and bulky stuff and to keep washing the diapers by hand. Every time I used it, I thought of your parents. And you."

Mrs. Xia's husband had died eight years before. The house on Fish Lip Lane belonged to her daughter and son-in-law. Her daughter's name was Yong-fang—Forever Fragrant.

I was sure that it was customary for a widow to live with her son. As if she'd read my mind, Mrs. Xia explained that she had lived for two years with her son's family in Zhenjiang, but things didn't work out with her daughter-in-law.

"It's better here, near the canal," she said. "Quieter, and my granddaughter is a delight. Sometimes," she added, "she reminds me of you."

Mrs. Xia insisted I stay for dinner with the family, and Yong-fang sent her husband, Lao Zhang, a city bus driver, to the market. After he returned laden with packages, I stood in the kitchen doorway watching the three of them busily preparing food. They chatted and gave each other advice and got in each other's way. But as soon as Dan-yang—Red Sunbeam—walked in the door, everything came to a stop. While Lao Zhang helped his daughter out of her worn and tattered backpack, Mrs. Xia handed her a slice of watermelon. Yong-fang disappeared and came back just as the introductions were winding up to announce that Dan-yang's bath was ready. Dan-yang left the room smiling, as if she was entitled to all the attention.

She returned just as the sizzle of meat in the wok and the fragrance of fried garlic crept in from the kitchen. Dan-yang's hair was cut short. She had changed into a light blue sundress and white sandals, a totally different style from her parents, who favoured dark trousers and white shirts. I warmed up to her a little when she began to tell me about herself. Three years away from university entrance exams, she was already worried.

"My parents remind me about the exams almost every day, since I started kindergarten," she complained. "Neither of them had a chance to finish high school because of the Cultural Revolution, which I am sick of hearing about. They want me to have what they missed."

She pointed to the stack of dog-eared books she had left on the table when she came home. "Those are extra studies. I take after-hours classes in math, Chinese, chemistry, and English. My parents want me to be a doctor, so I can take care of them when they become old like *Wai-po*."

I switched to English. "Is that what you want—to be a doctor?"

"I not want that," she replied awkwardly. "I hate the chemistry and never good at the math. I want to be teacher in elementary school."

"So, why don't you—?"

She switched back to Mandarin. "But I am the only child and they have high hopes for me. My parents gave me life and they saved money to pay for the extra programs like academic clubs, interest groups, and private tutoring to improve my English. I hated it at the beginning, but my resentment only made them sad." She stopped and cast a glance towards the kitchen. "Maybe being a doctor won't be so bad. Our universal medical system is falling apart. In the old days, going to the doctor used to be called begging medicine. Beg is what you have to do now in the hospitals unless you're rich. *Wai-po* has stopped going to get treatment for her arthritis. It costs too much. Don't tell her I told you." Dan-yang sighed. "I just hope I won't disappoint my parents. It's very hard to get into medical school."

Parental guilt trip, I thought. I know about that.

The meal went on for two hours. My Chinese held up fairly well. Mrs. Xia's Mandarin was hard to follow, but that of her daughter and son-in-law was clearer. Dan-yang's was precise.

Yong-fang and Lao Zhang found it hard to understand that I had been accepted by a university and I had made up my own mind as to what to study. "But is that what your parents want you to do?" Lao Zhang kept asking. I told him my mother and father left the decision to me.

Later on, when we were slurping away at bowls of thin soup, Mrs. Xia told her family about how she had met my parents, but only because I had mentioned it.

"But I still don't understand why you changed the records to show that Dong-mei was deaf," Yong-fang said.

Mrs. Xia looked at me, then back to her daughter. "For some reason the Tearless Girl won my heart more than the others. She was such a quiet baby. I decided to help fate. Most of the girls would spend their lives in the orphanage. Only a few would be taken by foreign parents. If Dong-mei was 'imperfect,' the officials would try to place her. Many of the adopting parents had a child, and the policy said that these people must accept a less perfect baby. It was easy to make up the false document. But there were so many others I couldn't help. I hated being in that position, playing god. Who gave me the right to pick and choose?"

"I can't believe that you kept such a secret from me, Mother," Yong-fang complained. "I would never have known if Dong-mei hadn't come today."

"You ought to know that the best way to keep a secret is to tell no one," Mrs. Xia said. "I learned that lesson more than once in my life."

Later, Lao Zhang and Yong-fang insisted that I stay with the family while I was in Yangzhou.

"You've travelled thousands of miles, just like Dr. Bethune when he came from Canada to help China's revolution," Lao Zhang said, his chin quivering. "Staying in a hotel will be an insult to us."

"Thank you, but the man at the hotel desk will be looking for me," I said. "I told him what time I'd be back and I'm already late."

Besides not wanting to impose on the family, I was anxious to get to my room so I could phone home. Finally, Lao Zhang gave in, but insisted on taking me back to the hotel. I sat behind him on his bike, balanced on the rat-trap carrier as I had seen many others do on the streets. It was kind of fun. He let me into the hotel only after I promised once more to return the next day.

Mom answered the phone on the first ring. I talked to everyone, her, Dad, Megan, repeating the good news: I had found Mrs. Xia. I didn't tell them that my attitude to the family hero had changed completely.

I was ready to hit the road shortly after breakfast, but I had to wait until the hotel's gift shop opened. I bought a pair of fur-lined gloves for Mrs. Xia even though the radio had warned that the temperature would climb to 35 Celsius. Next winter they would warm her swollen fingers, I hoped. At the suggestion of the shop clerk, I bought a bottle of mao-tai, a strong rice wine, for Lao Zhang. "It's the best gift for a man," the clerk said, eyeing the bottle enviously. For Yong-fang I picked out an olive-coloured silk blouse. As for Dan-yang, I ended up buying a large backpack with a waist belt. I hoped my present wouldn't result in her taking more courses because she would have more room for books.

Before I headed out, I put Chun-mei's note in my pocket, promising myself that, somehow, I would get all the answers to all my questions by the end of the day.

"*Chi-fan-le-ma?*" Mrs. Xia greeted me when she opened the door. "Have you eaten yet?" is a Chinese way of saying hello. Soon we were back in the rattan chairs, sipping tea from large cups with lids on them. Yong-fang and Lao Zhang had taken the day off, in honour of my visit, but they were nowhere to be seen. Dan-yang had gone to school. I waited for a polite time to put my questions to Mrs. Xia, but she beat me to the punch.

"So, Dong-mei, I know you want to talk more about your mother and you didn't get the chance yesterday."

I took out Chun-mei's note, laminated between two

plastic sheets to protect it from dirt and damp. "Mrs. Xia, I want to find Chun-mei." I didn't say "my mother." "For most of my life, when I thought of her at all, I hated her. I don't any more. Now I need to get some answers from her."

PART FIVE

❀

Yangzhou, Jiangsu Province

MRS. XIA

❀

(1999)

Somehow I knew that the woman who had left the note with her baby would come back. I had seen it happen before. Sometimes the mother would come alone, sometimes with a friend or relative. Mostly they walked around the block, circling the building. The bolder ones would approach the off-duty staff, asking for details, pretending to inquire for someone else, but their eyes, empty and desperate, gave them away.

The government's one-child policy has the same iron-fisted punishment for any who abandon their children. Both parents face a jail sentence of up to five years, not to mention the penalties their families will suffer. But in my twenty years of working in various orphanages, only once did I see a parent caught. The police were called in by one of our staff members. The mother was arrested, and the child was taken back to live with the family that hadn't wanted her in the first place. The child would have been safer if she had been left with us. I doubt very much that she is still alive.

I'm wandering. I do it more and more lately. Yong-fang gets impatient with me sometimes.

Unlike the others, Chun-mei walked straight through the front doors of the orphanage. It was the first day of winter by the lunar calendar. Winter in our region was usually mild, but not that year. It had been cold and dreary for weeks, and even when the sun finally showed its face, so did the bitter northeast wind. All we had for warmth were three wood stoves, but most of the heat went up the chimneys. We hung heavy cotton quilts over the doors to keep out the icy drafts. Every child was bundled to their eyebrows. I swear that if you had lain one on the floor she would have rolled away like a tumbler.

Luckily, it was I who saw Chun-mei come in, shoving the quilts aside and looking around frantically. She stopped as soon as she noticed me. She had a wild, distracted look about her. She wore a thin, oversized padded jacket. No scarf, no gloves. Her shoulder-length hair was a bird's nest. She carried herself as if crushed under a heavy weight, as if her soul had left her.

She rushed up to me, wringing her hands, looking this way and that. "I want my daughter back," she whispered. "Please."

The next thing I knew she had dropped to her knees in front of me as if I were a buddha statue in a shrine. Her shoulders shook as she began to sob. I grabbed her and hauled her to her feet, then pulled her into a laundry room nearby and closed the door behind us.

"Be quiet! Someone will hear you!" I warned her.

It was near feeding time and as usual "the choir" had already begun as the children cried for their dinners. Inside the laundry room, with its pipes wrapped in straw, it was chilly and damp.

"My name is Chun-mei," the distraught woman said, fighting back her sobs. "I brought my baby here one year ago. Her name is Dong-mei. I made a mistake. I'm here to take her home."

No one can imagine how I felt as I stood there, shivering, with that pitiful wretch. How could I tell her the truth, even if I were allowed? The baby had been adopted by a couple from another country. She was far away, as beyond the reach of her mother as if she had been on the moon. And, I admit, my pity was mixed with fear. If the woman revealed her story I would be in deep trouble with the authorities. The whole thing might come out, the note I failed to report, my falsifying the girl's health record, my secret visit to the Canadian couple's hotel room. I'd be finished.

So I told a lie. I cupped Chun-mei's tear-stained chin with my hand and said that the baby she was describing to me had never lived at our orphanage. She pulled free of my grasp.

"I don't believe you! You're lying!"

"Listen, you've got to keep your voice down! Do you have any idea what will happen to you if someone finds out why you came here? That you left your child on our steps? Do you realize what kind of trouble you and your family will be in?"

The word *family* was like magic. Chun-mei instantly went limp. Her arms fell to her sides. Her weeping and begging ceased, as if someone had turned a key.

"Believe me, your baby isn't here," I repeated. "You'd better leave now, before someone comes."

I led her out of the laundry room and down the hall to the main entrance. Before she went out, she turned, giving me a look that would melt stone. Then she disappeared behind the quilt. I followed her out to make sure she went away. I wanted to tell her the truth, to comfort her, but I couldn't. All I could manage were banal questions.

"Where are you from? Do you have far to go? Is there someone who can be with you?"

"Liuhe Village." That was all she said before she made her way across the busy street, towards the bus station.

I told this to the girl from far away. We were both in tears by the time I had finished. Lao Zhang, my son-in-law, had been silent all through my telling, squatting on his heels against the wall, beside the rooster he had been plucking for our dinner. He and my daughter had taken the day off and had spent most of the morning shopping and preparing the food. Fish, shrimp and sliced eel, and green leaf vegetables lay ready for the wok.

Yong-fang was weeping too. "That poor woman," she whispered.

"All this time," Dong-mei said, "she thought I might be dead."

"There was nothing more I could do."

"I understand."

"I have a few friends who are long-distance bus drivers,"

my son-in-law cut in. "They are familiar with the surrounding area, better than anyone else. It may take a while, but we'll find this Liuhe Village. That's a father's promise."

It was not the first time that my heart swelled when my son-in-law spoke.

Two days passed. Lao Zhang worked with one of his closest friends, Lao Huang, making quiet enquiries about Liuhe Village. Dong-mei was impatient as young people are; she was not old enough to have learned how to wait. My son-in-law, after the first day, tried to explain to her that, because Dong-mei was a foreigner, he had to make his inquiries discreetly to protect everyone involved, his family and friends, and me, as well as Chun-mei herself. Where foreigners are involved, our nation's history and our personal experiences have taught us to be extra-careful and to keep things below the surface.

So I asked Dan-yang to take a few days off school and go sight-seeing with Dong-mei. There were some Tang dynasty ruins nearby, a wasteland of toppled tombstones, broken columns, and traces of fountains sticking out of the weeds, with a few statues still standing. One of them has become very popular in the past few years, I am told. I never go there myself.

On the second day, while my son-in-law continued his search, we four women made preparations for another feast. Yong-fang, who gets nervous at such times, anxious that everything turn out well, was running in and out of the kitchen like a chicken whose head has been chopped off, while the real chicken with its head still on marinated in our small refrigerator. Dan-yang was assigned to remove the pin feathers from a duck, grumbling to herself as she sat on a low stool, holding the duck under water in a basin as she plucked. Ordinarily I would have done the work, but my eyesight fades more every year.

Dong-mei seemed squeamish. When I asked her what was bothering her she told me quietly that she didn't like to see dead animals. I laughed. "Where do you think your food comes from?"

"From the supermarket," she answered, staring at the fish that swam in circles in a basin at her feet.

"What about fish?" I asked her.

"Well, I like it. But when we buy it, there's no head or tail or skin or bones. I remember one time when I was little. We were having fish and I found a bone in mine. I thought it was a miracle."

So I set Dong-mei to shelling peas. She seemed to find it fun and chatted away to the three of us, giggling like a child when a pea or two leaped from her fingers and rolled across the kitchen floor. As she worked, the light from the window fell across her figure. She was a beautiful girl, much taller than her mother, but her eyes were Chun-mei's. Her clothing was as bright as a bird's feathers, and new. I wondered once more what had become of her mother, whether Chun-mei had had a son, and, if so, if this lovely young woman from Canada was prepared for what she might find in Liuhe Village.

It was late afternoon. The food was ready to cook and we sat outside on a bench by the door, sipping tea and trying to catch the breeze from the canal. Passersby nodded to us, and stared without comment, probably wondering what on earth was going on in my household. We were laughing, smiling, chattering to each other in Mandarin. Among us was a stranger in stylish clothing. Our neighbours probably thought she was a long-lost relative.

"Dan-yang," Dong-mei said to my granddaughter, "why do the *hu-tongs* around here have such funny names?"

"Remember Emperor Yang Di, the cruel tyrant who was dragged from his throne?"

"The one who completed the Grand Canal?"

"That's him. The legend says when he was captured his enemies wrapped him tightly in the skin of a freshly killed leopard. As the skin dried, it slowly suffocated the emperor."

"Yuck. You didn't tell me that part. But what's that got to do with the street names?"

"I'm getting to that," answered my granddaughter, who, like her father, loved to drag out a story. "It was one of Yang Di's officials who decreed that the streets in this area should be named after delicacies that were served to the emperor at court, like bird's nest, shark's fin, swallow tail—"

"And fish lips," Dong-mei cut in, giggling. "I don't think I'd like to try those!"

I began to regret the special dish we had planned. But I had no time to warn Dong-mei, for Lao Zhang careered down the lane towards us and hopped off his bike, red faced and excited. "I have news!" he called.

Yong-fang hurried into the house, returning with a cool glass of beer. It was unusual for men in our area to drink beer, but Lao Zhang had been introduced to it by his friend at the bus station. My son-in-law was like a small boy who had been promised a new toy.

"I had no idea there is more than one village named after the Liu River," he began, taking a swallow of his beer. "At least four of them. Lao Huang and I agreed that two look promising. Between the two of them, which are about thirty miles apart, the one to the northwest of here looks best. There is no bus stop at either village, which is one reason why it took so long to locate them."

"When can I go?" Dong-mei interrupted.

My son-in-law was proud of his work for Dong-mei. He wouldn't be rushed.

"You probably wonder why we think the northwest one looks like the best bet," he said, smiling.

Dong-mei was a clever girl. Visibly hanging on to her impatience, she asked, "Why?"

"The one to the northeast, though closer to Yangzhou, is on the other side of the river, so villagers have to take a short ferry ride before they can catch the bus into the city. Your moth— Chun-mei had just given birth and it wasn't easy to travel in her condition, not to mention carrying the child with her. Besides, Lao Huang has mentioned the ferry terminal is right at the entrance to the village, so she would have been spotted by other passengers. Too much of a risk, see?"

Dong-mei nodded. "You should have been a detective instead of a bus driver," she said.

Lao Zhang grinned. "Anyway, my friend and I agree we should try the northwest Liuhe Village first. Lao Huang estimated it's less than two hours' bus ride, then about twenty minutes' walk from there to the village. If that's not the one, we'll go to the others, one after another. But remember, Dong-mei, it's a long shot."

"Can I go tomorrow?" Dong-mei asked. "I can take a taxi and get there faster."

"No, you can't," my son-in-law said firmly. "If you beat the grass, you'll frighten the snake."

"Daddy, stop talking in riddles!" Dan-yang said. "Dong-mei isn't familiar with all your old-fashioned expressions." Turning to Dong-mei, she added, "He likes to read old novels, and they are hurting his brain."

"If you go by taxi, you'll bring too much attention to yourself," my son-in-law explained. "It's better to enter the village on foot and make quiet inquiries. Even then you'll cause a stir."

"Okay, I'll take the bus. I leave early in the morning," Dong-mei said thoughtfully.

"No, no. That's not a good idea," I cut in. "We'll go with you. We don't want anything to happen—"

"But if all six of us barge in on the place," Dong-mei said with a smile, "that will be beating the grass, won't it?"

The determination on her face allowed no opposition. While she and Yong-fang and Dan-yang chattered excitedly about her trip the next day, I went into the kitchen to begin the meal. Lao Zhang followed me. He had planned a special dish for Dong-mei, whom he was already very fond of. Watching him busy preparing, humming tunelessly, I didn't have the heart to stop him.

GRACE

❀

(1999)

It was one of the best times I had ever had, and my stomach bulged from a feast of chicken, duck, vegetables, shrimp, steamed rice, and sweet cakes. Mrs. Xia's family treated me as one of their own. I sensed she felt some sort of obligation to me. But I think she liked me, too.

The big meal had gone slowly, with lots of conversation, jokes, and toasts that made my head light. Lao Zhang told a story from a Ming dynasty novel, using a high-pitched Beijing Opera style of voice that hurled Dan-yang and me into fits of laughter. And then Yong-fang, who I had thought was kind of shy, sang while everyone except Mrs. Xia tapped their chopsticks on the edge of their bowls. When Lao Zhang got up from the table and disappeared into the kitchen, Dan-yang insisted that it was my turn.

So I sang a twangy country-and-western tune, the-crops-failed-and-my-wife-left-me-and-my-pickup-truck-broke-down kind, making fun of the song. They looked at each other with raised eyebrows, probably wondering, What kind of music do they *have* in Canada? It was at that moment that Lao Zhang rushed into the room, carrying yet another platter steaming with the delicious aroma of ginger and garlic. God, I groaned inwardly. Not more food! He plunked it down on the table, right in front of me.

"What the *hell* is that?" I screamed.

I was staring into the wide, startled eyes of a live fish. It gazed back at me, opening and closing its mouth and pumping it gills, as if it had been rudely awakened from a nap. The body had been cooked and sliced into bite-sized morsels and piled behind the head. I realized with horror that it was the fish that had swum around in the basin earlier that day, and that its head was alive though its body was ready to eat.

"Am I hallucinating?" I exclaimed, again in English.

Confusion at the banquet table. Mrs. Xia said something sharply to Lao Zhang in local dialect and his face turned red. Dan-yang burst out laughing, her hand covering her mouth. Yong-fang looked frightened—for me or for the fish, I wasn't sure.

"It's called Still-alive Fish," Yong-fang said quietly. "It's a delicacy."

I had committed the biggest faux pas of my life. Lao Zhang had cooked a special dish in my honour, and I had ruined everything. Yong-fang reached across the table and turned the oval platter so the fish's head was no longer facing me. "It used to be served only at the imperial court," she added lamely.

"In ancient times," Lao Zhang put in, desperately trying to salvage the situation, "the cook would be beheaded if the fish arrived at the table and its mouth was not moving."

As if that helped.

Mrs. Xia rose and lifted up the platter. Before she could turn to take it away, I touched her arm. "Please, I want to try it. I bet it's delicious."

Mrs. Xia hesitated before putting the plate down. My eyes welled up. "I can never thank you all enough for your hospitality. I wish my dad were here. He would finish this dish all by himself." I picked up my wine cup, the old way I had learned from Frank, in both hands. "To my new-found friends in China," I said. "*Gan-bei!*"

I phoned home that night. My parents were happy that I was moving in with Mrs. Xia, until I told them there was no phone in the house and the public phone at the end of the lane didn't have overseas service. Early the next morning I checked out of the hotel and moved my stuff to Lao Zhang and Yong-fang's house. The night before, the whole family had ganged up on me, telling me I must stay with them. Where? I wanted to say. The house consisted of a small kitchen, a closet with a chamber pot, a sitting room, and one bedroom. Lao Zhang and Yong-fang had the bedroom, and Dan-yang and her grandmother slept in the living room. I wasn't looking forward to living in crammed surroundings, without a square foot to myself, but I felt I couldn't refuse. In a way, I told myself, I'd be a step closer to my goal.

I had put a lot of thought into the outfit I would wear to Liuhe Village. I didn't want to attract any more attention than necessary—or "beat the grass" as Lao Zhang would have put it. I had had no idea when I left home that Chinese women, even the younger ones, didn't wear shorts. They preferred skirts, dresses, or long pants, and blouses rather than T-shirts. So I was glad that Mom had insisted that I pack two dresses. The one with the floral pattern had a swooping neckline, so I opted for the beige linen, a loosely fitting dress that fell to just above my ankles and had a crew neck. I took off my cork sandals and put on a pair of running shoes. But when I looked at myself in the mirror I changed my mind again. The reflection reminded me of the career women in downtown Toronto during rush hour. I ended up in a pair of flat-heeled walking shoes.

Wishing myself good luck, I left the house and took a local bus to the long-distance station, where I would make the connection for Liuhe Village. I met Lao Zhang inside and followed him around the small, crowded terminal to a dilapidated contraption that looked like it had been built several dynasties back: a faded blue bus with a peeling white stripe. There were already passengers on board, looking bored behind the dirty windows.

Lao Zhang introduced me to his friend Lao Huang, who sat behind the wheel. He was a rough-looking character with a bristly crewcut. He smiled when we shook hands.

"This isn't my route," he said, "but the regular driver owed me a favour. Besides, no one cares who drives what, as long as the wheels are moving."

Lao Zhang laughed, then took me aside. "Listen, Dong-mei," he said, his voice suddenly serious, "let's hope your journey today will be successful. But you should also prepare yourself for disappointment."

I nodded. "I have."

"Good." Turning to his friend, he called out, "Take care of her!"

Lao Huang waved me into the seat behind him, which he had saved for me with a scuffed vinyl bag. Then he pulled the lever to shut the doors and started the engine.

The bus rumbled through the dusty outskirts of the city and into the flat countryside. Lao Huang kept up an almost constant stream of chatter. Like Lao Zhang, his accent was thick and I had to listen carefully over the hammering of the diesel engine. He was fascinated that I, a foreigner, could carry on a conversation in Chinese. A few of the passengers were eager to know about Canada, and tossed in questions wherever Lao Huang left an opening. A lot of their questions were personal and nosy by North American standards.

"What a smart *Ya-tou* you are!" Lao Huang called out repeatedly. The term in general means a slave girl or a young maid but was also a pet name used by a father to his daughter, or an uncle to his favourite niece. He meant well, but I wasn't thrilled with his choice of words.

Most worrisome were his comments about my mission, which he made at the same volume as his other remarks. "They will be so sorry, when they lay eyes on you, *Ya-tou*," or "They will pay for what they did to you in their next lives."

Finally the flood of questions from my fellow travellers ran dry, and I had a chance to look at the countryside and to try to take my mind off what lay ahead for me. Paddy after green paddy separated by narrow dikes stretched to the horizon, criss-crossed by ditches and larger waterways. The day was scorching by now, the air thick with humidity, the road sending off shimmering waves of heat.

The sun was high in the sky when Lao Huang pulled to the side of the road, under the shade of a few spindly poplars. A few people got off, hauling bundles, baskets, and live chickens in bamboo cages. An old couple climbed on. The bus jolted into motion with a roar of the engine—and made a U-turn.

Voices soared in protest. Lao Huang shouted, "I know what I'm doing, don't worry! I just have a small detour to make, then we will all be on our way!"

The hubbub went on. One old lady in a threadbare white shirt and black pants shouted and waved her fist.

"Will you be quiet?" Lao Huang yelled back. "I promise we won't lose any time. Now sit down and don't bug me." To me he said, "I am trying to save you the long walk to the village."

He swerved onto a bumpy side road, stirring up a tower of dust. Roosters and chickens squawked and shot to the side or flapped valiantly over the low mud wall that lined the road. A goat stood panic-stricken in the middle of the track until Lao Huang blasted the horn, and it bolted out of the way. The bus came to a stop before a square of cement, which had been swept clean. On one side stood a wall of bundled straw.

"The threshing ground," Lao Huang explained, getting out of his seat. He pointed. "Follow the path over there. It looks like it leads into the village. I will be back here around three o'clock. Don't be late, *Ya-tou*. Good luck."

I got down from the bus under the silent stares of the

other passengers. Lao Huang swung the bus around in the narrow road and roared away, trailing a cloud of yellow dust.

If I had expected to see farmers bending to their work in the lush green paddies on both sides of the path that led to a cluster of buildings, I was wrong. The fields were empty, the rice stalks swaying in the hot breeze. Gradually I approached an orderly collection of houses. The yards in front of the identical two-storey buildings were deserted. Chickens wandered around, pecking at the ground. Goats, chained to stakes, dozed in the shadow of overhanging clay-tiled roofs.

I was hot and sweaty and thirsty, and my ears were still ringing from the bus motor. There was a soggy patch under each of my arms and I could already feel the perspiration gather between my shoulder blades under my backpack. I began to regret my choice of a light-coloured dress. I stopped in the middle of the road. On my left a radio was faintly playing Beijing Opera. I heard people talking. Women's voices. I followed the sound and found myself standing outside an open door. A bike was propped against the wall.

The interior of the house looked cool and inviting. Inside were a large square table and a few benches. The hard-packed dirt floor had been swept clean. No one was in sight. My hands shook as I cleared my throat and called out a greeting. A young woman about my age, with a bowl in one hand and chopsticks in the other, came out of the back room. Judging from her pink blouse, black skirt, and white plastic sandals, she was a city woman, not a farmer.

"How do you do?" I said.

"Who are you looking for?" she asked warily, her mouth still full of rice.

"Who's that?" came a shrill voice from the rear of the house.

"I am looking for Chun-mei," I said calmly, sounding more confident than I felt.

"I don't know any Chun-mei," the young woman answered. "What's her family name?" She scooped more rice into her mouth.

"Um, I don't know."

"Then I can't help you."

"Is this Liuhe Village?" I asked when she began to turn away.

"Yes. But I don't know any Chun-mei," she repeated with irritation. "How old is she?"

I took a wild guess. "In her forties."

"Let me ask my mother."

The older woman walked towards me and stopped in the middle of the room, squinting. "Who are you?" she demanded. She was middle aged, chubby and strong, her face and hands deeply tanned. Beside her, her daughter looked pale and skinny.

"I'm a relative. I haven't seen Chun-mei for a long time. I was told she might live here."

"You're her relative but you don't know her last name?" the older woman said. "And you don't speak our dialect. Are you here alone?"

I began to get the feeling she knew the answer to my question but was reluctant to admit it. Her daughter put her bowl and chopsticks down on the table with a clatter. "Mother, if you know this Chun-mei woman, why don't you tell her? My lunch break is over. I have to go."

And she walked out of the room while her mother continued to look me over.

"Please, Aunt," I addressed her in the common term of respect, "just tell me if Chun-mei lives here. I didn't come to make trouble for her."

The woman kept silent, her mouth working as if she was making a decision. "Chun-mei used to live here, but not any more," she said.

My voice cracked. "Do you mean she's dead? Tell me!" I demanded when I got no answer.

"Come inside," she said, glancing up and down the path, her voice less harsh, "and sit for a minute. Chun-mei left the village a long time ago, the same year my daughter was born. That's how I remember."

Now that the woman had decided to talk, there was no stopping her.

"She and Loyal were a good match, at least that's what we all thought at the time. But it didn't last long. Less than three years. It was the first divorce in the village and surely set a bad example. I never heard anything of Chun-mei since. By the way, her family name is Ma."

Ma Chun-mei. Chinese women don't change their names when they marry.

Her daughter passed through the room, looped the strap of her purse over her shoulder, climbed on the bike, and pedalled off.

"Now, I've been honest with you. Return the favour," the

woman said, leaning her elbows on the table. "You're no relative or you'd have known she is a Ma."

"I am Chun-mei's daughter, Aunt. I live in Canada. She doesn't know I'm here. I don't want to cause any trouble."

She stared into my eyes, as if studying a map. "You can't—" she began. "How could—?" Her eyes widened and she slapped the tabletop. "*Aiya!* You're the girl who they said was stillborn! The one supposed to be buried in their vegetable plot! I always knew something wasn't right. *Aiya!* Power is a strange thing. It comes and it goes. Maybe you'd better think about what you are doing. People here always think twice before they deal with the Chens."

Who were the Chens, and what did power have to do with it? But I got her last line clear enough. She was giving me the brush-off.

"By the look of you, your family must be rich. Everybody in your country is rich, aren't they? So let well enough alone. Go home. Chun-mei isn't here any more. And if Firecracker finds out I've talked to you there will be no peace for me or my family. Not to mention Old Chen still has influence."

"Can't you at least tell me where Chun-mei has gone, or the name of her former husband?"

"You mean your father. He's here, all right. But I doubt he'll tell you anything, not without permission from Firecracker, and he isn't likely to get that. When Loyal married her, he lost his tongue." She peered into my face again. "All right, I'll tell you where the Chens live, but promise you won't say anything about me."

So Firecracker was Loyal's new wife. She sounds like a real scarecrow, I thought as the woman walked me to the door. But who was Old Chen? Keeping to the shadow of her room, she pointed up the road.

"Second row from the front, the last house on the left. Next to the vegetable plot with the bright yellow flowers," she said. "His name is Chen Zhong, Chen the Loyal. That makes you a Chen, too."

Her words spun in my head. Was I really so close to my destination? And what was all that babble about a baby buried in a vegetable plot?

My stomach churned as I made my way along the path. A part of me wanted to stop and think, maybe go back and ask the woman more questions so that I could somehow find Chun-mei without confronting new people who certainly didn't sound like they would welcome me. I couldn't have cared less about this Loyal guy, father or no father. It was clear to me that he had never wanted me. His name was not on the piece of paper Mrs. Xia had given to my parents. And Chun-mei returned alone to the orphanage a year later. But at the same time I was curious to see what he looked like.

And, I suddenly realized, I was metres away from the place where I had been born, in a little village, remote, backward, and poor. The people here had gone on with their lives after I had left the scene, totally unaware that a girl unwanted here had grown up in Canada, with a sister and two parents. I decided to screw up my courage and confront the man who had fathered me.

The houses in this part of the village were a little bigger but of similar design—two-storey brick, clay-tiled roofs, metal window frames. They reminded me of the townhouses in Milford. I was hungry and thirsty, but the orange pop and waffles in my backpack remained untouched.

Like all the houses I had passed, the one the woman had directed me to had its door open. This must be a safe neighbourhood, I thought. It was about one o'clock by then, and the whole village seemed to be napping. My heart hammered in my chest.

I reminded myself of Mrs. Xia's advice. "There is no use being bitter, Dong-mei. What happened to you is long in the past. And remember the elbow only bends one way. A family threatened by an outsider will draw together."

It was her way of reminding me that, as far as my birth family was concerned, I was someone else, an outsider. Not just a foreigner, but an unwanted child. Standing at the doorway, I hesitated, my courage slipping away from me. Maybe I'll wait a while until nap time is over, I thought. I wandered aimlessly through the village, past small plots cultivated between the rice paddies and bursting with beans and cabbages, along a canal where ducks floated serenely in the sun. The zzz-zzz of cicadas was loud in the heat.

A motorcycle roared into the village and stopped in a cloud of dust outside Loyal's house. A guy about my age shut off the engine, balancing the bike with splayed legs. He had a strange haircut, long on top, like some Hong Kong actors pictured outside the theatres in Toronto's Chinatown. Behind him was a young woman, her head and face covered by a colourful scarf, tied at the neck. She wore stylish, snug-fitting jeans and her ribbed shirt was so tight it divided her plump body into rings, like a sausage.

I heard a woman's voice. "Come on in. You must be hot.

Watermelon is ready." Her voice was rough, with an accent I didn't recognize.

Quiet returned to the village as the two young people got off the motorcycle and went inside. I walked gingerly past the door, but no one was in sight. And then, whether from the heat, the tension, or confusion, I lost my courage completely. I looked at my watch. In a half-hour, Lao Huang would be at the threshing ground with the bus, waiting for me. I shouldn't be late, especially if he had a bunch of passengers as grumpy as he had had earlier that day.

I decided to call it quits, at least for that day, and walked to the threshing ground. I sat on a tree stump in the shade and gulped down a bottle of warm pop. An old man walked past with a pole over his shoulder. On each end of the pole was an empty bucket.

"Good day, Miss," he said. "Hot day, isn't it?"

"Yes, it is, Old Comrade," I replied, standing up.

"Are you waiting for someone?" he asked.

"My friend is picking me up."

"You're not from around here," he said. "You speak Common Language. Are you visiting someone?"

"I came to visit the Chen family, but I ran out of time, so I'll come back tomorrow."

He pushed his straw hat back, revealing a shaved, deeply tanned head. "The Chens," he murmured.

"Yes." I tried the subtle approach. "I haven't met Firecracker, though."

He laughed. "Never call her that to her face, young miss. If you do, she'll show you how she got her name!"

❀

When I stepped down from the bus the next morning, Liuhe Village seemed a different place. There were people about, unlike the day before, and as I headed nervously to the Chen house a small crowd followed me, women and men, a few kids, a number of seniors, all yakking away in the local dialect, pointing to my backpack, my clothing, my hair.

The motorcycle guy, as I had come to think of him, was standing in front of the house. He ducked inside when he saw me approach. I stopped at the doorway and looked in. Lying on a chaise longue made of bamboo in the centre of the room was a middle-aged woman. The motorcycle guy slouched beside her, giving me a cold smile. One of his front teeth was missing and the corner was chipped off another. Under thick brows, his narrow eyes were far apart.

He came towards me, putting out his right hand. "I am Ah-miao."

His name meant seed. I shook hands with him. The woman sat straight up on the edge of her chair, her eyes locked onto mine, her bare feet slipping into a pair of sandals.

"My name is Dong—"

"I know who you are," she cut me off, jumping to her feet. She had a broad face, with high cheekbones and full lips that would have combined to give her a playful look if her face was not clouded with anger. Her shoulder-length hair was tightly curled, and bounced when she moved. I heard the crowd behind me shuffle back from the door. The woman stopped inches from where I stood and said loudly, "I also know that you have been snooping around behind our backs." Spit flew from her mouth, narrowly missing me.

I took a breath, holding back my anger, willing myself to speak slowly to avoid misunderstanding. "I am not snooping around. My name is Dong-mei and I came here to look for my mother. Her name is Chun-mei. If you know anything about her, I'd appreciate your help. If not, maybe there's someone else here who is willing to give me some information."

The woman's hostility wasn't nearly as much of a shock as the realization that, for the first time in my life, I had called Chun-mei my mother.

Two men had appeared at the doorway that led to the back of the house. One, whom I could see clearly, was short and broad-shouldered, wearing a T-shirt that may have been white once but wasn't any more. He stared at me, his eyes wide. Beside him, half hidden, was a taller, older man. He held one hand to his face. The skin on the back of his hand was wrinkled and deeply tanned. He quickly ducked out of sight.

Whether the shorter man wanted to say something I didn't know, but he didn't get the chance because the woman whirled around and lit into him. This must be Firecracker, I thought as soon as she began to shriek.

"You useless turtle's egg! Didn't you tell me your daughter was dead? Come on!" she barked, pointing at me. "Take a good look! Maybe she's a ghost come to collect you and that stupid old man hiding behind you!"

So the guy in the dirty T-shirt was my birth father. Our eyes met for a second before he looked away, shaking his head. Ah-miao had sat back down. His eyes shifted between Loyal and me. He smirked, as if enjoying the show.

"And you!" Firecracker shouted when the old man showed himself again, looking straight at me. His face was a map of wrinkles. He had on a black shirt without a collar, and baggy pants. Although his shoulders were stooped, he was one of the tallest men I had seen since coming to China. His goatee was pure white. "Stupid donkey!" Firecracker raged. "Here's your dead granddaughter, here to summon you to hell. What are you afraid of, you self-appointed hotshot?"

The old man stared at me, ignoring the woman's tirade, then turned and vanished once again.

I realized the old man must be my grandfather; Firecracker I knew was Loyal's second wife. Did that make the smirking motorcycle guy my half-brother? One big happy family.

I had once asked Frank in our class how to swear in Chinese. He had refused to tell us. After we pushed him harder he sheepishly said that the worst thing you could say was to insult your opponent's mother. Firecracker had mastered her cursing well, and even though she used quite a few local terms, I had little trouble following her.

"You wanted to see a big show for free," Firecracker screeched at the villagers, whose number was increasing by the minute. "Then piss on all of you! And piss on your mothers!" Her arms flailed, her spit flew, her feet stamped on the cement floor in rhythm with her shouting. But she didn't notice Loyal coming up behind her. He grabbed her roughly by the shoulder, spun her around, and slapped her across the face so hard her head snapped back.

Ah-miao scrambled to his feet and took one step. But

Firecracker could not be stopped. Her screaming intensified. "You useless shit-head! That's all you are, wife beater. You're not going to treat me the way you treated your first wife!"

"Where is she?" I broke in. "Can't you stop all this and tell me where she is?"

Firecracker and Loyal looked at me. I began to shake and tears ran from my eyes. "Damn you!" I cried out. "Damn all of you!"

"What is she talking about?" someone in the crowd whispered.

"She's a foreigner," said one of the women. "The poor thing. She came all the way here from Canada to find Chun-mei. But it's too late."

I spun around. "You mean she's dead?"

"It's too late," the woman repeated.

PART SIX

❀

Liuhe Village, Jiangsu Province

OLD REVOLUTIONARY CHEN

❀

(1999)

I knew it. I knew something bad was about to happen. My left eyelid had been twitching for days. My dear wife, who was taken from me seventeen years ago, used to say, "Left eye, catastrophe; right eye, luck."

I am glad she was not there to witness this; it would have killed her all over again. I tried to convince myself that my old head was playing tricks on me. Did I hear it right? That lovely young woman who stood tall and straight as a poplar in our front yard is my granddaughter?

One single slip can cause a lifetime of sorrow, my wife used to say. She had warned me many times. When it turned out that Chun-mei was no longer her daughter-in-law and Firecracker was going to marry Loyal, her poor heart gave up on her. She told me with her last breath that I would be punished, if not in this life, in the next. I didn't believe her then. If there was a medicine that could cure regret, I would cross a sea of fire and climb a mountain of knives to get it. I'm over eighty years old, toothless and aching in every joint. My body has gone downhill, but my memory is as keen as the edge of a sickle.

I wish I would forget that December evening nearly nineteen years ago. It was the moment I led my family down the path to hell.

My daughter-in-law's pregnancy had gone well, although as her father-in-law I didn't make direct inquires. Loyal's mother filled me in. Loyal had given me a detailed report of Old Fu's prediction. Since then, I would often laugh myself awake from my dreams, imagining my grandson playing at my feet, or bouncing on my knee.

I showed due respect to my daughter-in-law, more than tradition required. Through old connections and past influence, I was able to arrange light jobs for her instead of field work. Later, an opening came up in a local factory, folding cardboard boxes, and I got her the position. She was the envy of every young woman in her condition. No more exposure to the wind and rain and sun, no standing on her feet all day. Loyal had been a sickly child who gave me many nights without sleep. I wanted my grandson to have a strong start, right from the beginning.

What a dirty joke it was! My supposed grandson turned out to be a baby girl! If the child had been delivered in the county hospital, according to my daughter-in-law's plan, I would have fought and argued all the way to the central government in Beijing, accusing the doctors and nurses of switching babies on me. It wouldn't have been the first time in this country. But when the time came, one frigid evening of freezing rain and snow, I urged Loyal to go and get Sister Liu.

"It will be a very uncomfortable journey for your wife, lying in the wagon, pulled by the walking tractor. The hospital is too far and the roads are too slippery."

Loyal hesitated.

"Trust me. I know what I'm doing," I said. "Just remember, you and your sisters were all born at home. You don't think I would take a risk where my grandson is concerned, do you? Your mama and Sister Liu have brought enough babies into the world to make up a platoon."

So Loyal rushed out into the storm to fetch Sister Liu.

Hours later, when I was told the disastrous news, I pounded my fist on the closed door of the bedroom where the mother and her useless newborn lay, screaming through the planks at that Liu woman, whom I thought I could trust, then at my wife. Loyal paced the floor behind me. He had wanted to be with his wife, but I wouldn't let him. I had to remind him that men should stay away from childbirth. Too much blood, unclean blood, which would bring bad luck to men.

Loyal urged me to calm down. What was going through his mind I couldn't say, but his behaviour, and the look on his face, destroyed my trust. I had to come up with a plan, and soon.

Sister Liu, I knew, wouldn't be a problem. She and her whole family were indebted to me for help I had given them during the years when I was in office. Nor would my wife be a worry to me. But my daughter-in-law caught me and Loyal off guard. I had heard rumours when I was looking for a wife for Loyal that she was headstrong, but she was a young woman, I had told myself, nothing I couldn't handle. Ever since she joined our family she had never shown me, Loyal, or my wife the slightest disrespect. That night, though, she showed her true colours.

My plan fell apart almost as soon as it had been hatched. It depended on getting the baby away from its mother, out of that room. But my wife stupidly let the mother hold the baby. Sister Liu failed me, too. She should have stopped my wife from making that mistake!

Loyal, too, was useless. That brain of his, usually his pride, turned to bean curd. When he finally went into the room, all he did was scurry back and forth between his wife and me, acting as a messenger. "She won't give the baby up," he kept repeating. "What am I going to do?"

I hadn't seen Loyal look so helpless for years. He hadn't asked for my advice for a long time, not since he got his big ideas about building a new house and starting up a business with those pathetic rabbits. I had taken his change of heart as a sign that he had learned his lesson, his way of putting me back as head of the family again. It was past midnight and we had to act fast. I had never underestimated his wife's intelligence, but I had surely misjudged her ability to cause damage.

"We've got to come up with another plan," I told my son.

What a night that was. A storm overhead and freezing rain coating the countryside with ice. My wife in bed, facing the wall and refusing to speak to me. Me sitting on the edge of the bed, smoking one cigarette after another. My daughter-in-law weeping in her room as her and Loyal's voices rose and fell. My son, the seed of Chen, running in and out of the room, wringing his hands.

I had never dreamed that I would one day bargain with my daughter-in-law, a disgrace unheard of since Emperor Chin united China. Nor was I happy to see my son turned into a parrot, repeating her words and mine. But a deal was finally reached hours after dawn.

Loyal brought me her final words. "Tell your father he can inform the village authorities that my daughter was stillborn, or whatever story he wants to make up. But if he tries to hurt her in any way, he will be sorry he ever drew breath in this world."

I was shocked. I had no idea this usually soft-spoken woman with her gentle manner could utter such hateful and disobedient words. But I felt badly for Loyal. He seemed aged overnight, his face drawn, his shoulders hunched. So I agreed.

During the next two days only my wife was allowed into the room to be with the mother and child. She had tried to get me to look at what she called the lovely baby. While to everyone in the village I was a tough old bird, my wife knew my weakness. I had to remind myself not to lay eyes on the child. I had to be strong at the critical moment of my son's life, to make sure he had another chance to get a son.

Time dragged. The freezing rain gave way to wet snow that shut down the village. People stayed at home, keeping warm. I had asked Loyal to hang quilts over the door and to cover all the windows in the same manner. I pretended it was to keep out the northeast wind, but my real concern was the baby's cries. She was a fierce little thing, I'll say that for her. But her racket was an enemy to my plans.

Early on the morning of the third day, Loyal walked into our bedroom and said, "She's gone." I could hardly see him because dawn had not yet arrived. After he said those two words, he left. I lay still, staring into the darkness. Beside me, my wife began to weep quietly. She had been in bed most of the time since the baby was born, when she was not looking after the mother and child. She had complained of chest pains and she needed rest. Only months later I learned that she hadn't been well for quite a while.

What a day that was. No one stirred from bed until noon. Our chimney stayed smokeless all day and the house was a cold dark cave, as if we had already fallen into hell.

That afternoon I lay down for a nap, exhausted by the tension of the past days, the silence around me, the lack of sleep. I could not feel the relief I had hoped for. I must have dozed off. I was awakened by the sound of uncontrolled sobbing. I got out of bed, followed the sound up the stairs, found the two women crying. I saw Loyal's wife lying on her back, facing the ceiling, her clothes rumpled and her hair in a tangle, and Loyal standing at the foot of the bed as motionless as a tree stump. My wife sat on the edge of the bed, her eyes red and swollen. She looked up, saw me, then looked away. My wife of forty years was suddenly a stranger.

"Go away!" my daughter-in-law shouted as soon as she saw me. Her face was twisted with pain. She pointed at me. "You heartless animal! You will pay for this before you die." Then she let out a loud cry so sad and broken it would soften a stone.

That was the last time Loyal's wife spoke to me. During the month-long confinement my wife cooked and washed for her like a hired maid, and when the confinement was over she went back to work in the factory right away. I didn't need my wife to tell me we had a stranger living under our roof now. Gone were the smiles that had come so easily to my daughter-in-law's face, and her respect towards me and Loyal. When I came near, she would cast down her eyes and ignore me.

Gradually, as the winter wore itself out and spring came, she softened a bit towards Loyal, and I was pleased to learn that he was back sleeping in the same bed with her. This time, I promised myself, there would be no trips to see that fool Fu. If I had to, I would sell every chicken in our yard, even the two pigs I was raising, to pay for a visit to the machine that had eyes to see through a woman's belly.

If I began after that terrible winter to feel hope again, the hope turned to shame, and my household, once one of the premier families in the village, became the focus of rumour and ridicule. My poor wife never recovered from not knowing what had happened to the child she had helped to deliver. But the arrival at our home of Qiu-xiang, a woman we had never heard of, killed her. While her ashes were still warm, Loyal was forced to marry the brash and ignorant woman from Sichuan Province. At their wedding dinner I couldn't hold back my tears, and when Qiu-xiang caught me wiping my eyes, she exploded in anger, thus earning her nickname, Firecracker.

Ah-miao, Loyal's son, was born five months later, but there was little joy for me. No matter how hard I tried, I couldn't pretend the happiness I didn't feel. My son's new wife sensed my true feelings, and from that day became my enemy. If we had been a dragon and a tiger in our former lives, she told me one day, we were cat and mouse now. She meant one of us must die if the other was to live in peace. By then my dear wife was gone and the thought of joining her didn't sound too bad. Then one day it dawned on me that I did have something to look forward to: to watch my grandson grow tall and strong. So I refused to die.

I have committed my share of sins. But I, too, have a belly full of bitterness. As far as this Chun-mei business goes, when all is said and done, I was desperate. I wanted to be a good citizen, to obey the rules of the government, to do my small part in building the new China. I rose to high office in the brigade and I was widely respected as a good and honest official. I followed the Party line and Chairman Mao's instructions when he was alive and continued to do so after his death.

I can hardly express my shock and heartache when I learned recently that while the Chairman had called upon the people of China to pull down the remnants of the rotten bourgeoisie, he himself went through one marriage after another, with more wives than I had pairs of shoes. Worse, it was said that for two decades before he died he had kept a pretty young country woman in his chamber, day and night, while his new wife lived only feet away. My jaw dropped when I saw the recent photo of her in the newspaper. Yet Chairman Mao wasn't the only one of my idols to be toppled like a tombstone. Premier Zhou En-lai and his wife were once widely admired as a childless couple who sacrificed family life to serve the Party and socialist China, who claimed that the children of China were their own. It turned out that Zhou had fathered a daughter with another woman. Loyal showed me a book written by that daughter. Her photo was on the cover. She was the image of the Premier. The daughter as well as her mother had been visited many times by the Premier and his wife.

Lies piled on lies. White turned to black, black became red. In my village, families of Bad Elements, a class defined and attacked by the government for more than three decades, were praised by the same government when they got rich investing in non-farming business. They made so much money that they were able to hire poor labourers from Anhui Province to work on their land while they bought themselves cars. In the country where we peasants had thrown off cruel landlords and made a revolution, now the landlords were back!

But I couldn't complain, not when bourgeois attitudes could be found in my own family. When Loyal's scandal came to light he thought I would kill him for sure, but I didn't make much fuss. I even surprised myself.

I couldn't help feeling betrayed. I had been fooled and played with for so long that I excused myself for what I did to Chun-mei and the child. If that's a sin, so be it. No, I suppose I am no better than the next man, but I am no worse either. Or so I had convinced myself after these many bitter years, until my granddaughter came all the way from Canada to look for her mother. In her determination I see the spirit of the Chen family, the spirit I thought I had thrown away.

LOYAL

(1999)

Chun-mei and I had never been lovers like the ones in those Hong Kong movies. We married first and fell in love later. At least, that's how I felt about our relationship.

We had planned that our baby was going to be delivered in the county hospital. It was Chun-mei's idea and I agreed, even though it was unusual in both her family and mine. My stodgy father accused me of seeking change for its own sake, but I thought, if my wife is more comfortable in the hospital, why not?

During her pregnancy, while I referred to the unborn child as our son, Chun-mei always called it our baby. Once I asked her why, considering that Old Fu had made a clear pronouncement on the matter. She gave me the first and only superstitious answer I ever heard from her. "You can spit out a mouthful of rice because you took too much, but you can't unsay the words you've uttered." It was her way of saying, if you call the baby a boy you will tempt Fate to fool you. She sounded like my mother, not my wife.

The night of the birth I noticed the fear, almost horror, on Chun-mei's face when Father sent for Sister Liu. Chun-mei begged me to take her to the hospital, to stick to our original plan, never mind the ice storm raging outside, and the cold, and the prediction that we would have snow after the freezing rain. She ignored Mother's warning that she was well into her labour, that the water had come, whatever that meant. I saw no cause for her fears, but I had also learned that pregnant women were not the most logical creatures in the world.

Even to this day I can recall with dread the screams passing through that closed door. Each one tore my heart. I wanted to be with Chun-mei, but tradition strictly forbade it. I wanted to go outside and walk the paths of the village, but the weather made it impossible. I felt as if I was trapped in a pen. My father was no help. He paced around, upstairs and downstairs, inside his room and out again. When his hands weren't fidgeting, scratching his forehead or rubbing the back of his neck, they found brief refuge in his sleeves.

When the baby's cries echoed in the house, his eyes lit up like lanterns and my heart soared. I forgot my wife's discomfort. My father clapped me on the shoulder. "Listen to his lusty bawling!" he said with a laugh. "A chubby little boy for sure!" But there were no sounds of celebration behind that door. When the baby quieted there was only silence.

"What's going on?" Father shouted, pounding the door with his fists. "Bring out my grandson."

There was no response. The light left my father's face, and I myself was overcome with the dreadful feeling that something had gone wrong. Then the door cracked open, revealing my mother's drawn features and desperate red eyes. No baby lay in her arms. Behind her, my wife wept weakly among tangled sheets, as if the screams I had heard only moments before had drained the life from her.

"There is no son, my child," Mother murmured, sadly shaking her head. "It's a girl." Then she closed the door.

"It has to be a mistake," I said, pushing open the door. Sister Liu, her shoulders hunched as if she expected a blow, scuttled behind me out of the room. I heard my father's angry words.

I walked around the bed and stared down at Chun-mei and the tiny bundle resting in her arms. I reached out to the blankets to see for myself the gender of the child, but Chun-mei hissed, "No! Don't touch her!" Her words were like knives; her face twisted with—what? Not hatred. A kind of animal defensiveness that made it clear she would die before giving up that child.

Numb with confusion and guilt and grief, I ran up and down the stairs all night carrying messages between two strong-willed people who had become enemies. Each time I entered the room Chun-mei clinched the child closer. Though she was so tired that opening her eyes was an effort, her head was as clear as spring water and her voice was firm as she stated her conditions. If she could keep her baby, she would indebt herself for life to pay the fine when she became pregnant again; she was willing to have her allotment of land taken from her; and she would go away, stay in hiding, until the second child was due and safe.

My father would not agree to anything she suggested.

He sat on the edge of his bed, smoking, shaking his head. She must hand over the child. That was his bottom line. I carried his threats to my wife. I couldn't believe how her beautiful eyes had turned so cold, how her sweet modest voice had grown so hard.

"If you harm my little girl I swear I will give you and that old man no peace until I die. In case you have forgotten"—she let her words out one at a time—"I am the daughter of a landlord, a survivor. There is not much for me to lose. Leave us alone, and give me two more days. I promise Dong-mei will disappear from your lives. Go tell that to your old man. There will be no more talk."

She closed her eyes then and turned her back to me. She had called the child Dong-mei, as if she had known all along it would be a girl. Winter Plum-blossom fit with her own name, Spring Plum-blossom.

Chun-mei kept her promise. Two days later, when the snow and ice had melted away, she left the house before dawn and returned after dark, without the child. She walked in the door and went straight to our room without saying a word. No one dared to ask her where she had gone and what she had done with the baby. My father's relief was visible on his face. My mother was silent and glum. For my part, I tried to look ahead to the future.

Next day, my father sent Sister Liu to Chun-mei's village to make quiet inquiries. She reported that there was no sign of a baby living in her parents' household. "From what I could gather," the old midwife and matchmaker said, "the Mas have no knowledge of the newborn. They are preoccupied with their business as well as caring for the King of the

Salted Egg, who is ailing. Badly, they say," she added. Chun-mei's father had suffered a stroke three months after our marriage, losing his ability to speak. He had been bedridden ever since.

When he received the news from Sister Liu, my father smiled for the first time in days. "It's better this way," he said to me. "Time will pass and heal the wounds. Then you and your wife can try again."

Meanwhile, the whole family, especially me, had to put up a front. It wasn't a matter of pulling the wool over others' eyes. For the past couple of years people in the village had stopped asking questions when a newborn died, especially if it was a girl, as if an understanding had formed among the villagers. There seemed to have been a sharp increase in the number of stillborn girls. Some choked on their own vomit, some were accidentally strangled by the cord, some just stopped breathing, as simple as that. In the cities, I had heard, a doctor had to be present, a death certificate made out. Not in Liuhe Village.

So when it was my turn to put together a small wooden box and bury it in our vegetable plot, I received the usual condolences and sympathy. The strange thing was, I did feel as if my child had been born dead.

My wife endured her one-month confinement without me, keeping to the room, sleeping or staring out the window. Her meals were taken up to her by my mother. Often the food went untouched. I slept in the storage room at the back of the house, alongside the farm tools, sharing a wall with chickens and pigs.

On the day when the monthly confinement was over,

Chun-mei emerged from her room. Her clothing was twisted and wrinkled, she gave off a sour odour, and her once shiny hair was a mess. She walked straight to the village barber and had it cut off shorter than mine. When she saw the three of us staring at her, goggle-eyed, she laughed. But it wasn't her old laugh. It was cold and bitter. The next day she went back to work.

My father had said that time would heal her loss, but for my wife time offered no solace. A month later, just after the Lunar New Year, which marked our first wedding anniversary, Chun-mei's father passed away. I accompanied her to Poplar Tree Village and helped with funeral arrangements. Her family knew no more about what had happened that December night in the Chen household than anyone else. So far as I could see, the whole thing was behind us, or buried in that wooden box.

This time, it was Chun-mei who had to put up a front. She sat beside me on a bench during the funeral service, next to her mother. Once, she took my hand during the eulogy. It had been a long time since I had felt the touch of her skin. When the three-day mourning period came to an end she told me, to my surprise, that she was going home with me, not staying with her mother. I had been worried that she might use the funeral as an excuse to stay away from me and my family.

But when it came time to leave, her grief broke my heart. She was in tears before we stepped out of the house, and every two steps she took, she ran back three. She wailed and cried and fell on her knees in the middle of the road, asking forgiveness from her dead father.

"There is nothing to be forgiven, my dear child," her mother comforted her. "Your father knew you were busy with your work and family duties."

She didn't add "and your pregnancy and dealing with your own loss." But the words hung in the air.

That night, back home, was the first that Chun-mei allowed me to lie beside her. But she kept silent with her back to me. I heard her weeping in the dark and mumbling in her sleep. We both tossed and turned until dawn broke.

When spring arrived, my wife's spirits lifted somewhat. Her pallid skin took on some colour and she walked with a lighter step. She grew her hair out a bit, although it was still short, and some of the girls in the village copied her style. One day, on my way home from the market, I passed her workroom at the factory and saw her laughing with a co-worker, her head bent back, her face up to the late afternoon sun and her hair catching the light. I swore she was the most beautiful woman on earth. I would have given anything if she would share that laugh with me.

To everyone in the village, Chun-mei was herself again. When the May Day Fair was held in the town market, I wasn't surprised that she was chosen as Queen of the Fair. She was dressed in red robes with a metal crown on her head, and paraded through the streets in a wooden cart pulled by a donkey festooned in red bunting. Young girls, lined up to be "received" by her, the Queen, shrieked with excitement, and new mothers with babies in their arms chatted while waiting their turn. When one of them pushed her baby girl onto Chun-mei's lap, saying she hoped her child would grow up to be as beautiful as the Queen, Chun-mei blanched, thrust the child into her mother's arms, yanked off the metal crown, and ran away.

Half a year passed before Chun-mei and I became husband and wife again. I dared to be happy again, but gladness is never pure. I couldn't stop thinking about my duty to plant a child. Around that time I read in a magazine that it was the husband, not the wife, who determined the gender of the baby. I could hardly believe it. Our tradition was to blame the mother for a girl, praise her for a boy. What an awful discovery that was!

I didn't need any magazine to tell me that anyone could make a baby. Look at my parents. Neither one could read or write, but they had produced half a dozen kids, no sweat. Practice was all that mattered. That was what I kept in mind all that summer and far into the autumn. Considering Chun-mei's track record—she had gotten pregnant less than a month after our wedding—she ought to have had good news right away. But there was no sign. I was getting anxious but didn't dare let it show.

Eventually suspicion grew in me like a snake. I knew all about having fun without making babies. Birth control was drummed into everyone's head, old and young, by the government. Chun-mei and I were not controlling anything, as far as I was aware. But just to be sure, I visited the brigade's clinic where condoms and pills were given out free of charge. I persuaded the assistant to let me check the ledger, which listed the comings and goings of the patients and their treatment and prescriptions. Chun-mei's name wasn't there. I also paid a visit to the doctor, an old crony of my father's, and he promised to tell me if Chun-mei ever showed up asking for birth-control stuff.

And then one Sunday afternoon, in early October, Chun-mei had to go to work at the factory to finish her quota. I decided to tidy up our bedroom, hoping to impress her. When I pulled a clean sheet from the top shelf of the wardrobe, a package tumbled down with it. The fine print on the label said "avoiding pregnancy pills." A few were missing.

I shook with rage. Chun-mei was lucky that she wasn't around. She had been cheating me, and my family, destroying my dreams, leaving me and my father with no heir. Hours later, I heard her footsteps in the house and shouted for her to come upstairs. When she saw the silver package I was holding, she turned pale.

"Tell me you haven't been taking these," I demanded.

She didn't answer right away. She walked to the window where the sun's rays were disappearing below the horizon. "Yes, I've been taking them," she said calmly.

I grabbed her sleeve. "Who gave them to you?"

"No one. I got them myself."

"Liar!" I shouted. "Tell me the truth!"

I raised my hand but caught myself just in time. When she saw that, the steely look she had given to me on that December night after the baby was born reappeared.

"There is no more to tell," she said and left the room. She quickly returned with a big basket full of the baby clothes she and her mother and my mother had made during her pregnancy. She pulled out blankets, tiny shirts, sweaters and cotton-padded jackets and diapers, flinging them onto the floor. Five more boxes of pills flew into the air.

"There are more here. Do you want to see them, too?" she sneered, tossing a box at me. "Or would you rather have a look at some of Dong-mei's unused diapers?"

She cast a handful of the cotton squares against my chest. I stepped forward and grabbed the collar of her blouse, twisting it into a tight knot. "Why are you doing this to me!" I screamed.

"Because I won't give you or your father another baby to kill."

I slapped her hard across the face. Chun-mei took the blow silently, her eyes flashing. I heard a gasp behind me. My mother was standing in the doorway.

"What have you done, Loyal?" she hissed through trembling lips. "The devil finally got you, didn't he?"

Chun-mei stood where she was, the welts caused by my fingers rising on her cheek. With her sleeve, she wiped away a trickle of blood at the corner of her mouth. There were no tears in her eyes. I too had become her enemy.

This time it was Chun-me who moved out of our bedroom. She set her bed in the nursery that would never be a nursery, a couple of planks resting on two benches. To outsiders, our household remained normal. Chun-mei left for the factory each morning and sat with us at the supper table every evening. After helping my mother to clean up the dishes, she disappeared for the night behind the closed door of her room. Occasionally she spoke to my mother, but to me and my father she was as silent as a ghost. I tried a few times to make up, but she ignored me, and when she did look at me her eyes were blank.

One November day, when I was waiting to get my

pushcart repaired at the town market, I met Qiu-xiang, a young woman who worked at a noodle stand. It was more than her strange accent that got my attention. She was not pretty, but pleasant enough, with a saucy provocativeness that made my heart itch. After that I made sure to pass the noodle stand each time I was in town. She was very friendly to me, and gave me extra noodles, sometimes meat, and chatted with me, all smiles and compliments.

Where she used to live, she told me, was ten times poorer than our area. She and her friends, who were sharing a room nearby, had travelled a long way to get here, taking up jobs that the locals didn't want, hoping to be able to save up for a hope chest, essential if they wanted to get husbands.

The first time she invited me to her place I was shocked and turned her down immediately. She teased me about being shy. "We're both grown-ups," she said, giving me that look that brought sweat to my forehead. "I won't bite you."

Eventually I gave in, starting with short visits. We'd sit on the edge of her bed, listen to music and talk, and drink a little rice wine. Then we began to lie down side by side. Soon I spent the night with her, once a week, then twice, and more. Sometimes her friends were around, but Qiu-xiang assured me that the three of them had reached a mutual understanding when it came to visits by men.

I insisted that she take pills. To save her the trouble and embarrassment of going to a clinic, I brought her the boxes that had belonged to Chun-mei. Why not, I said to myself. She had no use for them. Most important, it was my way of showing her that, just because the tailor who lived at home wouldn't sew for me, it didn't mean I had to wear rags.

One chilly December day as dark was falling I came back from town to find my mother waiting for me at the threshing ground. She was bundled up against the cold, a scarf wrapped around her mouth.

"What's happened, Ma?" I asked.

"Chun-mei didn't come home from work. We haven't seen her since this morning."

It turned out Mother had gone to the factory when Chun-mei didn't come home at her usual time, and discovered that my wife hadn't turned up for work at all. She'd been gone the whole day, and no one had seen her.

"Don't worry, Ma," I told her. "She might have gone back to Poplar Tree Village. I'll go there tomorrow if it will make you feel better."

"I'm not so sure about that," Mother replied. "Do you remember what day it is today?"

I had no answer.

"I thought so, a *busy* man like you! It was a year ago today that Chun-mei gave birth to your child!"

Chun-mei came home a few hours later. The three of us watched silently as she walked into the house, bringing in the bone-chilling northeast wind. If I had met her on the street I wouldn't have recognized her. Her face was expressionless; her eyes were two empty holes. She had on an old faded jacket of mine that I hadn't worn for years. She passed by the table where we were sitting, leaving the door open behind her, and climbed the stairs.

My mother got to her feet and followed. My father buried his face in his hands as if the silence was too much for him. I hadn't mentioned what day it was, and I said nothing now. But I knew the cause of Chun-mei's behaviour.

The scream came, from the back of the house, after I had gone to bed. I ran downstairs and threw open the back door to find a clutch of my neighbours staring up at the second-storey window.

The double window of the nursery was wide open, and Chun-mei stood balanced on the sill, looking down at the crowd. A scarf was gathered around her neck and she had on the same tattered jacket. The chilly wind whipped her hair around her face. Her arms were held in front of her as if she carried a bundle. She began to sing, gently swinging her arms sideways.

I shouted at her to get down, conscious of the eyes of the gossips near me. But Chun-mei put one finger to her lips and said quietly, "Shhhh, you'll wake Dong-mei." And she continued her song.

I dashed into the house and ran back upstairs to find my father standing behind Chun-mei, pounding his fist into his hand in frustration. My mother, her body shaking uncontrollably, was begging Chun-mei to step down. As if it were not enough humiliation to last a lifetime, eventually I had to ask two of my neighbours for help, because Chun-mei screamed each time I tried to approach her. The two men coaxed my wife from the window.

My mother and Sister Liu cared for her, bringing her tea and food, but not before I had tied her to the bed frame by her wrists and ankles.

Some of the neighbours couldn't resist comments as they pretended to console me. "She ought to have nerves as hard as steel," said one, "considering what she and her family have gone through in the past."

"I always thought landlords and their kind were a bunch of ruthless, cold-hearted people," offered another. "Going out of your mind over a baby girl, dead for a year? Unheard of."

Chun-mei, the clinic doctor told me, suffered from "nerve sickness." There was no mental hospital in our area. The nearest, in Yangzhou, about thirty miles away, had a long waiting list, and city residents got priority. Chun-mei would have to be cared for at home, like most of the mental patients in the village. In her case she had to be watched twenty-four hours a day so she wouldn't hurt herself. His words left me nothing to look forward to but caring for an insane woman for the rest of my life.

Four days later, Chun-mei's mother and elder brother showed up at our door. I took them upstairs, and when my mother-in-law saw Chun-mei tied to the bed like a caged animal, she broke down. And Gen-fa was all business. He had taken over the salted-egg company and become head of the family after his father had passed away.

"One of our relatives is a doctor in a hospital in Zhenjiang," he said quietly, staring at the dishevelled bundle on the bed. "I have contacted him. He may be able to pull a few strings to get my sister the treatment she needs. Of course you and your father will agree to let my sister come home with Mother and me."

His words might have sounded humble and polite, but the tone made it clear he would not accept a negative answer. And why would I say no? The truth was, I felt a wave of relief bear me up. How could I help my wife, after all? Even if she were sane, she wanted nothing to do with me. No, it was better all around if she went away. I admit to a pang of fear that she would tell her brother the real story about what had led to her illness. Or even worse. But, I reasoned, Gen-fa wouldn't believe her. Once a mad woman, forever insane.

My mother was heartbroken watching Chun-mei's brother settle her in a "turtle cart," a three-wheeled motor car. Less than a week later, Mother suffered a stroke that left her speechless and partly paralyzed. Although I was busy looking after my ailing mother, I did make an attempt to see Chun-mei, but when she caught sight of me she flew into a rage. When she was hospitalized, I tried again, but the doctor warned me to stay away. He said my visit interfered with the treatment.

The new year of the rooster brought no joy to our morgue-like household. I thought many times that I must now be at the lowest point in my life and that things could only get better, although how they would improve was anyone's guess. Two days into the new year, I heard a woman shout my name outside our door. I recognized her voice immediately.

I pulled the door open, dumbfounded. I hadn't seen Qiu-xiang for about two months. My mother, who had been sitting in a chair beside my father, wrapped in blankets and soaking up the sun by the window, stared intently at the strange woman. Qiu-xiang was no longer the slender little thing I remembered. The buttons on her padded coat strained against her swollen belly.

"Hello, Loyal."

I said nothing. My father threw a withering glance my way. Mother kept gazing at Qiu-xiang, her toothless mouth sucking in and out like a bellows, her hand pressing her chest, breathing hard as if she couldn't get enough air.

"Not much of a welcome here for the mother of your child," Qiu-xiang said brashly.

"Keep your voice down," I urged. "What are you doing here?"

"Isn't that obvious? And don't talk to me like that. It's time for you to live up to your responsibilities. This is what happens when you play in flour when your hands are wet."

PART SEVEN

Poplar Tree Village, Jiangsu Province

GRACE

✿

(1999)

The towering poplars that gave the village its name lined a straight dirt road that led to a cluster of houses in the distance. Under an overcast sky, the leaves of the trees quavered in the sultry breeze. In the branches, the cicadas buzzed rhythmically, and at my feet puffs of dust rose as I walked.

Farmers in the paddies straightened their backs, their eyes following me. As I approached the buildings, men and women and kids began to gather. News of my journey to Liuhe Village the day before must have reached here. There were no camera crews and nobody pushed a microphone into my face, but they had been waiting for me. Behind and beside me voices called out, "*Ta-lai-le! Ta-lai-le!* She's here! She's here!"

Loyal had given me directions—grudgingly, as if it had cost him money—to my uncle Gen-fa's, house. A larger group of villagers blocked a narrow path that wound its way to a dwelling that stood apart from the others. They stared at me as they silently stepped aside, allowing me to pass. In my mind I heard myself say to Mrs. Xia the night before, "I wonder if Chun-mei is still alive," and her reply, "I'm sure she is. Otherwise Loyal would have said something." But I had learned already that Loyal couldn't be relied on too much.

A tall man stood at the door of Gen-fa's house, formal, almost at attention. Despite the heat he was wearing a Mao jacket over a white shirt buttoned to the neck. His hair was neatly combed straight back from his forehead.

"Are you Ma Gen-fa?" I asked.

He nodded. His adam's apple bobbed once.

"My name is Dong-mei. I've come to find my mother."

He said nothing. If he was surprised to see me, he didn't show it. His eyes never left my face. He stood motionless, as if making a decision.

It had all come down to this moment, my long journey from the little girl who hated all things Chinese, through the hours of language lessons, through the growing yearning to find out where I had come from, to meet and challenge the woman who had thrown me away. I had walked the paths of the village where I had been born, met some of the family and neighbours I would have grown up with. And now I stood at the door of a house, speaking to a man who was my uncle, and I knew as sure as the harsh buzzing of the cicadas in the trees that he held the last piece of the puzzle.

He pointed to the door. "Please," he said.

Inside, a woman sat on a low stool with her back to me. As I came closer, I saw that she was spooning porridge into the mouth of an old lady sitting in a wide bamboo chair. The woman feeding her was younger. She was wearing a yellow shirt that showed her thin arms, and black pants with the legs rolled up a few inches over her ankles. Her long hair hung down her back in a single braid.

As if she sensed my presence, slowly she turned. Our eyes met and locked. The hair at her temples had turned grey. Lines creased the corners of her eyes, but I knew them right away. They were my eyes.

My lips began to tremble and my throat thickened. I felt weightless. The woman stood up and the bowl and spoon fell from her hands.

"It's you," she said quietly.

I nodded. She murmured something to herself, something about flowers and water, but I couldn't make it out. Then she raised her voice.

"You've come back to me. I've been waiting."

"Me, too, Mom," I said. "Me, too."

CHUN-MEI

❀

(1999)

My father loved books and flowers. When I was a little girl I would slip into my parents' bedroom and run my fingers along the spines of the books, history, literature, and philosophy, lined up on the three shelves beside the big rosewood bed. And when I was old enough, five or six, I can't remember, he would tell me the stories he had read while we were tending the peonies and planting them in big pots by our door. My brothers had no time for books, so my father read only to me at nights, before I went to bed. I was glad my brothers were uninterested. It made our time special.

My favourite was a novel called *The Scholars*, and the part I liked best was the poem at the beginning.

> In our lives
> we walk different paths.
> Generals, statesmen,

saints, even the Immortals
start out as ordinary people.
Dynasties rise and fall,
morning fades to evening.
Winds off the river
blow down trees
from former reigns.
Fame, wealth, and rank
vanish away.
So do not crave these things,
Wasting your days.
Drink up and be merry!
Who can tell
where the waters carry blossoms
cast upon them?

During the dark years of the Cultural Revolution, flowers were declared bourgeois trash, and people caught growing them or displaying them in their windows were hauled away to struggle-meetings and publicly criticized. I remember the day my mother watched horrified as Father tore the peonies from the pots and threw them on the compost heap. "What will you do?" she asked him. "We'll keep the seeds," he said.

Books, especially novels from the old days, were labelled "poison weeds" and burned. My father was forced to turn over all his precious volumes and watch as they were tossed into a roaring bonfire the Red Guards lit on the threshing ground. This time I was the one to ask, "Dad, what will you do without your books?" He managed to put up a smile and tapped his temple. "We'll keep the seeds," he told me.

So I tried to hold in my head as many of the stories he had read to me as I could, but as I grew most of them faded away. But not that poem.

Long before I was married I thought I had learned what human beings could do to one another. All through my childhood and young womanhood my family was spurned and spat upon because of the government policy. The campaigns against landlords, capitalists, and rightists seemed never to end, and my family's "dirty blood" put us on the wrong side every time. There were things that went on during the Cultural Revolution that would curdle a person's blood, dirty or not.

But I was still shocked when I became aware that some people would do away with innocent babies, get rid of them because they were not boys. More than once I wondered why the gods didn't enable us women to keep girl babies inside us long enough that they could not be so easily hurt when they left our wombs. One time I found a dead baby on the roadside near our village, wrapped from head to toe in paper, like an undelivered parcel; another time, I saw an infant floating in the water, bumping against the foundation of the arched stone bridge over the Liu River. Both were girls. Yet they were not the worst.

Throughout the village were clay-lined pits, one for each family, where, because chemical fertilizer cost money, we composted our night-soil until it was ready to be spread on the paddies or vegetable plots. I was twenty-one the day I was coming home from the paddies, sore and exhausted from working all day knee deep in chilly water, bent at the waist, transplanting row after row of rice seedlings. My pole rested on my aching shoulder as I walked, and my calves and feet were numb from the cold. I passed the compost pit of a family that lived on the edge of the village. Something in it caught my eye and I stopped and looked in. A baby was half submerged in the dark liquid, its umbilical cord trailing from its distended belly.

When I told my mother what I had seen, my voice shook. I expected a shadow of shock and horror to cross her face, but she took it calmly. It was nothing new, she told me; "an old trick in a new time" were her exact words. No matter who was in power, she went on, nothing changed much when it came to making babies and giving birth. A baby was like property, a personal belonging. "In the old days girl babies were put away because of poverty, shame, or some other reason," Mother said. "Now, if you want a son and you have a daughter . . ."

"But in a cesspit?" I shouted, slapping the tabletop. "It's as if they were punished for being the wrong gender. If anyone should float in shit it's the people who would do that to a baby!"

My mother sighed. "Believe it or not, Daughter, in my day 'chamber-pot death' was well understood and accepted. And sometimes it *was* an accident. You'll find out, when you are married and pregnant, that when it's time to deliver and the contractions start it does feel like you have to relieve yourself. And it was also used as a lame excuse for killing unwanted babies."

"But the 'accidental' ones were always girls, weren't they?"

Mama said nothing. She nodded.

When my time came and my baby was on her way into the world, all those memories rushed back to me. It would have been different if Loyal and his father held the same attitudes to the gender of children as my father did. So I worked out a plan to deliver my child in the town hospital, where getting rid of a baby would be very hard. I pretended to be afraid of a home delivery, showing false faith in modern facilities and doctors. Loyal agreed. After frowning and letting it be known that the decision should have been his, so did his father.

The truth was I never liked the hospital, and felt sick to my stomach after my visit to the maternity ward, which was just a huge room filled with beds, thirty altogether, where the moans and cries of mothers-to-be competed with the wails of babies, and the air smelled of bodies and disinfectant. I also took a look into a delivery room, even though the sign forbade it. It was a much smaller room, four beds on each side. Five of them were occupied by screaming, sweating women. Their legs hung in stirrups, spread wide, their private places visible. I quickly walked away. I almost changed my mind right there and then about having my baby in that horrible place. But I reminded myself that if my baby was a girl, the more people who saw her arrive, the safer she would be. So I vowed that I would go through with it, even if the delivery room was as big and accessible as the threshing ground.

But like a straw roof rotted with age, my plans fell in on me and I had my baby at home. When my father-in-law sent Loyal for Sister Liu, not the tractor and wagon that would take me to the hospital, I panicked.

At work, I had heard other women talking about the pains that came before delivery, how intolerable they were, tearing your insides, and how quickly they left you and were forgotten once the child emerged from your body. That night, I experienced the opposite. After the contractions started, I worried so much I was numb to the pain. Not a word could get through my clenched teeth. Loyal's mother was upset and confused. "Breathe," she urged. "Shout, Chun-mei. Yell your heart out, as every woman does."

When my baby began to crawl into this world, my body half wanted to comply with what Sister Liu and my mother-in-law urged me to do. Push. Push again. Push harder. Endless pushing. The amount of strength I spent could have toppled a mountain. I was exhausted, but my mind was clear. On the one hand I wanted to end it. On the other, knowing Loyal and his father were waiting like crows outside, ready to celebrate or to murder, I wanted to keep the child inside me, protected. I wished Loyal could have been with me. Maybe if he witnesses my agony he would understand better. But he kept to the old tradition.

With one last push, I lost my baby to the world. Sister Liu let out a cry: "The child has come!" Though deadly tired, I raised myself up on my elbows and watched every movement my mother-in-law and Sister Liu made as they worked on my baby. Their silence told me everything. Loyal's father pounded on the door, demanding to see his grandson right away. Sister Liu looked down at me, then averted her eyes. My mother-in-law's hands shook as she wiped the baby with a cloth soaked in warm water, tears streaming down her face. Sister Liu wrapped my child in blankets, but it was my mother-in-law who picked her up, her eyes on the door that echoed with the knocking that grew louder with every blow.

"Bring me the baby!" my father-in-law demanded. "Let's see him."

Loyal's mother hesitated. Sister Liu held out her arms. I knew what was to happen. As soon as my baby was out of the room I would never see her again.

"Please," I begged. "Let me hold my baby. Just once."

"Not a good idea," Sister Liu said firmly.

I shrieked. "Give me my daughter! It's not her fault! Let her live!"

My mother-in-law pushed Sister Liu away from the bed and placed Dong-mei in my arms. Clutching the tiny bundle, I turned my back on the door, where the pounding rose like thunder.

My baby's perfection filled me with wonder—ten tiny tapered fingers and ten button-like toes, a head full of black hair, large eyes clamped shut as if she was shy. If I had hoped for only a second that her appearance would win her father over to our side, that hope faded with the departing darkness. I didn't dare let him near her. Once again Loyal slunk into the room, not to ease my pain or defend his daughter but to demand she be turned over to her fate. After hours of coming and going up the stairs to listen to his father's commandments at one moment and my distraught demands another, he and the old man came to realize that Dong-mei would not be given into their hands. The negotiations began. The husband I had grown to be fond of and could have come to love became an outsider, bargaining over his own daughter's welfare and survival. By dawn a deal was finally struck. If they would leave me and my child alone, I would make her disappear within three days.

I look back on those hours, wondering how other mothers would judge me. Not as harshly as I judged myself. I was at the end of my rope, alone and trapped. The only ally I had in the household was Mother-in-law, but she was on the sidelines, already in trouble for disobeying her husband. How could I protect my child when the two men were set in their plans, like dried clay? The minute my back was turned, I knew, something would "happen" to my baby girl.

Nor was running away an option. In my native village I would be easily found. My parents no longer had a home of their own. As was the custom, they lived with my three married brothers, one year in each household. They would all be shamed eternally if I returned to the village with a child. I would have to go far away, but where? The farthest I had ever travelled in my life was to the city of Yangzhou, thirty miles distant. If I escaped to the city I would be arrested and sent home because I had no residence papers. Nowadays people are more free to travel from one place to another. Not so when Dong-mei was born. Where you had no residence papers you had no status.

Maybe I didn't make the best judgment. But lying in my damp and soiled bed, exhausted and disheartened, I decided I had one choice and one choice only: to get Dong-mei far away from her father and grandfather, so that they would never find her. In order to save her, I had to give her away.

❀

My only first-hand knowledge of an orphanage was what the name means: a place filled with unfortunate children who had lost their parents. Nothing more, nothing less. On my shopping trip to Yangzhou before my wedding I had passed the place, a derelict and forbidding red-brick building close to the bus station. Of course at that time I never thought I'd ever pass through the big double wooden doors with the peeling green paint, although I did wonder whether my brothers and I would have ended up there if my parents had been executed like so many other landlords in the early years.

One day in the workshop, long before Dong-mei was born, one of my co-workers mentioned that since the new family policy had come into effect, orphanages all over the country had become dumping grounds, or "collection houses," for children who had been abandoned by their parents because they were deformed, disabled, retarded—or female. Police were usually involved trying to locate the parents but often failed, and the numbers of "orphans" had been rising rapidly. But the thought that one day I would be one of those parents didn't cross my mind then.

On the third day I crept down the stairs long before dawn and let myself out into the freezing dark. My baby was bundled so thickly with so many layers of blankets that she was truly a "candle parcel" as we say in our part of the country, and her little face was covered with a thin scarf. She hung in a sleeping sack around my neck, her head resting under my chin.

Not a single light shone in the village as I slowly made my way down the path, between the houses of my sleeping neighbours. Most of the snow had melted but the air was frigid and damp, and my breath soon formed a layer of frost along the edge of my cotton scarf.

I was light-headed, as if walking on clouds. At twenty-four years of age I was a healthy woman, and strong, thanks to a lifetime of hard labour in the fields. But the last few days had worn me down. The birth itself would have been enough, but the cut between my legs, which still burned and bled, and the strain of keeping Loyal and his father away from my child for the last three days, had taken a heavy toll. Only my decision to save my daughter kept my legs moving, but after a half-hour of walking, I began to fear that determination might not be enough to carry me through the journey.

If there ever was a god, something I had never believed because he hadn't been there when my family and I needed him most, I found him that morning. Thin, pale light was seeping into the landscape, revealing the forlorn paddies with frost-covered brown stubble and the black, naked branches of the trees reaching into a grey sky. I heard a truck behind me, and when it drew abreast of me, it stopped.

The driver, a young guy with a few wisps of hair on his chin, leaned out of the cab and asked me where I was going.

"To Yangzhou," I said simply.

He pushed his cap with the red star on it back on his head. People hadn't worn caps like that for years. "Hop in. I can take you there," he said.

Circumstances make us do things we would ordinarily push away. Accepting a ride from a strange man on an empty road was unthinkable. But I climbed awkwardly into the truck, relieved and grateful, for I couldn't have gone ten more steps. The young man drove silently, making no attempt to start a conversation. Occasionally he glanced at me and the quiet bundle resting on my lap. Only the engine made a sound throughout the trip. He let me off at the city's bus station shortly before seven o'clock.

My plan was to spend the day in the dingy waiting room of the bus station until darkness fell and I could leave my baby at the orphanage unseen. The fewer people who saw me, the better. But I had to be careful. I couldn't just park myself on a bench and doze off, or I would be noticed. I got up once in a while, walked around as if I was waiting for someone. I could hardly stay awake, even though the station was noisy with blaring announcements over the loudspeaker and busy with the tramp of feet going to and fro, the roar of bus engines outside the walls, the incessant din of chattering mouths.

In the late morning I had to go to the washroom. I had tried to put it off as long as I could. I got up off the bench and went through the door to the toilets. The stench was so overpowering my eyes began to water. I noticed right away that the doorless cubicles were so narrow I couldn't possibly take Dong-mei with me.

I returned to the waiting room, to the corner where I had been sitting, and reluctantly put my baby down on the bench, knotting her blankets to the slats. I rushed into the toilet, found an empty cubicle, and squatted over the ditch, trying not to breathe, hurrying myself. But my dressings were blood-soaked and I had to rummage in my pockets for the fresh strips of cloth I had brought with me. Moments later I heard yelling. I looked up and caught my breath. A woman stood in the doorway, holding up my baby, demanding to know who she belonged to.

A man's voice came from behind her. "It's one of those again, isn't it?"

"Looks like it." Another man.

"They're everywhere nowadays. In bus terminals, train stations, even in ditches. The poor baby girls. We got to educate these country people better!"

The woman marched in and stood in front of the cubicles. "Whose baby is this?" she asked again.

I don't know why I didn't call out immediately, but I had spent the day trying not to attract anyone's notice. I was squatting over a foul-smelling ditch, layering rags inside my underpants. I stood and pulled my clothing into place. "She's mine. I had to use the toilet."

The damn woman insisted on making an announcement. "I found the mother. The baby wasn't abandoned after all."

That evening, after dark, I made my way to the orphanage, left my daughter on the steps, and ran into the deepest shadows beside the building, weeping.

I would never have done what I did if I had known Dongmei was going to disappear. My thinking when I placed her on the steps that night was that she would be in the care of a government facility. I had heard that some city folks sent their children to boarding nurseries and schools, seeing them once a week or so. I hoped that in a few years the government might change its rules, as it had so often in the past, reversing this policy or that. I had less hope, but still some, that Loyal and his father might have a change of heart.

But when none of my wishes came true I lost my courage. I went back a year later to reclaim my child, ready to take whatever punishment the police might pile up on me as long as I could have her back. When I was told by a woman at the orphanage that my baby girl was not there, I broke down. She refused even to acknowledge that Dongmei had lived at the orphanage. She looked distressed when I mentioned the piece of paper I had tucked into Dongmei's blankets. I had the feeling she wanted to say more, but how could I read her mind when I was losing my own?

It was disgusting and hypocritical but no surprise to me when the commune leaders used my father's funeral as a show for the living. Such dishonesty was typical of our rulers at all levels. It was the government that carried out the political campaigns that almost killed my father and gave the rest of us a life filled with poverty and misery and ridicule. It was the same government that reversed things after Deng Xiao-ping came along with his talk of white cats and black cats, how it didn't matter what colour a cat was as long as it could catch mice. Suddenly men like my father, who had been cast down for their business sense and experience, were now praised and encouraged to do business, to catch mice.

As soon as the news came that Mr. Wang, my father's former business partner, was coming from Hong Kong to pay his respects, two officials turned up to take charge of the funeral ceremony. Even I knew that Mr. Wang and his father had fled to Hong Kong to escape Chairman Mao's government, and throughout my youth men like them had been called enemies of the state and capitalist traitors.

Now, here were the officials from the commune, spending hours gluing pieces of paper with names on them to the benches, then changing their minds, ripping them off and regluing them to different spots. They were trying to get the ranks in order. The hotshots ended up perching on their own names in the front rows, while behind them sat the mourning relatives and friends. The bosses turned my father's funeral into a monkey show. Nothing personal, everything businesslike.

While they were playing their political chess, I mourned not just the father I had lost but the child I had abandoned. I grieved for the evils I had committed, a mother who didn't stand up to protect her own child. Staring at the small wooden box that held my father's ashes, I recalled the bad years when he'd been forced to kneel on a pile of broken bricks for hours, hands tied behind his back, his head weighed down by a tall hat made of sheet metal. Eventually he fell forward and lay on the ground, but they didn't set him free even then. No matter how inhumanely he was treated by the kind of men who now took over his funeral, he never lifted a hand to his wife or children, or lost his love for us. His memory was like a reproach for what I had done to my own daughter. His death was my punishment. Everyone at the funeral took my overwhelming sorrow as grief for the loss of both my father and child. How right they were, and how wrong. But I couldn't share with anyone the truth, not even my mother.

The saying goes that time cures all wounds. "Eases" was

more like it in my case, for my wounds could never be healed. I tried my best to take up my life again, knowing nothing could be the same but willing to do my best. That was what Loyal and his father had expected. The day after I got back from Yangzhou, Loyal had already dug the phony grave and buried the "stillborn" child. It's there yet, I hear, covered with tall grass. It was his father's idea and as usual Loyal went along. Loyal would tend the grave occasionally, weeding the mound and adding dirt after heavy rains. I often wondered what he was thinking when he engaged himself in that stupid task.

When my one month's confinement was over, I went back to the factory. I had my hair cut off like a man and neglected my appearance. I couldn't care less if Loyal or any man ever found me attractive again. When I did return to Poplar Tree Village to see my mother, it was difficult. No matter which of my three brothers' houses I sat down in, the question was the same. Was I pregnant again yet? Each time I heard that word I could have jumped out of my skin. But how could I explain to my family that I didn't want to have another child? What if I gave birth to another girl?

I got the pills as soon as I could. I was well aware of the close relationship between the doctor at the clinic and the old man, so I went to a drugstore in Yangzhou after telling Loyal I was going to visit my mother. The pills there were free and nobody asked any questions.

It was just a matter of time, I suppose, before Loyal discovered my secret. In a way I was relieved. By then we had resumed the life of a husband and wife. He was disappointed each time my period came, but he tried to be patient. Yet when he found the pills he gave me no time to explain. His palm was too ready.

If the marriage could not go down the road he had planned, then for him it wasn't worth having. Shortly afterwards he began to spend hours away from home, then whole nights. By then I had moved into the nursery.

I don't remember anything about the night when I lost my mind, but I'd already felt that I was drifting away, as if sanity was a shore and I was in a rudderless boat carried out to sea by currents I didn't understand. I recall going home to Poplar Tree Village, and my stay in the hospital, and long days of confinement in the houses of my brothers. I drifted for I don't know how long. Then one spring I began to feel myself growing strong again.

From time to time news would reach me about my former life. I learned that I was divorced, and that Loyal had remarried and his new wife had fulfilled her assignment. Good for her. I never laid eyes on her or the boy, although people said she had a tongue as sharp as a sickle and just as hard. No matter. She's Empress Dowager now. She provided the Chens with an heir.

Sometimes hard labour is a blessing.

For the first few years after my brother brought me home, the people in our village shunned me, whispering behind their hands as I passed by, as if mental illness was contagious. Even my brothers regarded me as a woman who might fall back into madness at any time. They would not allow me to care for my niece or nephews for fear I'd hurt them. When she changed dwellings each year, moving from one brother's house to another's, my mother carried me with her like a damaged suitcase.

So I lost myself in the intense rhythms of farming. In winter we sowed wheat in the dry paddies. In spring we harvested the wheat, sending the bundles to the threshing ground, then flooded the paddies before transplanting the rice seedlings. I stood bent at the waist, knee deep in brown water, thrusting seedlings into the mud. We took two crops of rice off the paddies through the hot months, then drained them for the winter wheat.

I went to the fields every day. Afterwards, as the light faded, I chopped weeds in our vegetable plot and watered the melons, beans, and cabbages. The only break came with the Lunar New Year's celebrations, when the wheat in the fields and turnips in the gardens needed less attention. Gradually, as the years blended into one another, I was accepted again by the villagers, though never completely. I watched my brothers' kids grow as my mother declined. Before I knew it I was well into my middle age.

Then came the day when the village bristled with talk about a young foreign woman who had showed up in Liuhe Village, causing an uproar. More startling were the rumours about who she was, and her intention to come to Poplar Tree Village.

I dismissed the gossip. I had long since stopped being surprised at the nonsense some people would believe. Nor did I want to open old wounds with speculation. But in spite of myself I mulled over the words the woman at the orphanage had said to me. She had pretended Dong-mei had never been there. Was it possible my daughter was sold to a foreigner?

It made no sense, but the questions dogged me on the way to the paddies and all through the day and then on the walk home to my brother's house. So just like my silly neighbours, I, too, waited for the foreign woman to show up.

Nearly twenty years dissolved in one second. She arrived, standing in front of me, tall, healthy, and beautiful. Our eyes met and the empty place inside me filled with joy and happiness. My daughter. My lovely Dong-mei.

Before she left that first day to go back to the place she was staying, I showed her a watercolour that my father had given to me as a wedding present. The painting shows a black branch heavy with blossoms.

"But where are the leaves?" she asked in her strange accent. "There are flowers but no leaves."

"That is what makes winter blossoms unique," I told her. "They bloom while surrounded by ice and snow."

GRACE

❀

(1999)

In a way I felt cheated—finding my mother, finally, then realizing I had only four days before I had to leave China. So I spent the rest of my stay in Poplar Tree Village. You would have thought Chun-mei and I would use up the whole time talking our heads off, trying to compensate for nineteen years of lost time. But her three brothers, my uncles, didn't give us the chance. Each of them held a banquet at his house, with the same cousins and friends and neighbours at each feast, eating and drinking and singing songs, and insisting that I eat more, eat more! When I got home, I knew, I'd have to diet for six months to make up for the watermelon, baked duck, winter-melon soup, stir-fried vegetables, chicken, steamed fish, and the local delicacy, pig's feet stewed in soy sauce, with thick layers of fat and skin that the others chewed with noisy enjoyment. Not to mention pop and wine and cakes.

So Chun-mei and I talked in the evenings and mornings. She would sit across the table from me and hold my hands in hers, as I told her about my life in Canada. Chun-mei asked a thousand questions about school and my friends, my sister and parents. I could tell that some of my answers bewildered her.

Her mother, my *Wai-po*, sat on the couch as we talked. It was clear she couldn't understand what was happening around her, although her wrinkled eyes would occasionally shift between Chun-mei and me as if trying to make some kind of connection. Chun-mei told me the stroke *Wai-po* had suffered a few years earlier ripped away her voice and put her mind to sleep. "Two women in the same household whose minds can't be trusted," Chun-mei had said with an ironic smile.

Uncle Gen-fa had told me a bit about Chun-mei's breakdown after I made a quiet inquiry about her condition. "She's been steady, or normal, for a few years," he had said. "But my sister has changed greatly. She used to be a quiet woman, but determined. My father often said that when Chun-mei made up her mind, even nine water buffaloes yoked together weren't strong enough to change her decision. Now she is more passive. Maybe that's better. She's middle-aged now. There are no battles for her to fight. And yesterday, Dong-mei, I saw her smile. That is your doing. It was the first time since she came home from Liuhe Village."

I thought briefly about staying longer, but I would have to extend my visa, and to do that I'd have to go back to Shanghai, and there wasn't enough time. On the morning of my last day there, I said goodbye to *Wai-po* at the house.

Chun-mei and all my uncles and their families, and almost everyone in the village, it seemed, walked me out to the paved road where I could catch the bus. My youngest uncle, Gen-shen, insisted on carrying my pack, which was loaded down with gifts they had given me for Megan, my parents, and my grandparents. Chun-mei asked me again and again if I would come back, and each time I promised I would. I told her I might even come to China to study for a year or two. She was concerned about whether my Canadian parents would allow me. When we saw the bus down the road, floating in the shimmering heat waves that rose from the pavement, despite my decision not to do so, I put my arms around Chun-mei. She didn't push me away. She held me tight and said softly into my ear, "Goodbye, my beautiful daughter. I'm in peace now at last."

I wasn't on the bus for long. I had promised Ah-miao I would return to say goodbye to him and his mother before I left for Canada. Although I had mixed feelings about it, I wanted to keep my word. I didn't, though, expect to see a full house waiting for me. Everyone was there, Ah-miao, Qiu-xiang, Loyal, and his father. I still couldn't bring myself to call Loyal my father or his father Grandfather. I had nothing but contempt for both of them.

Qiu-xiang was the one I felt sorry for, stuck with a husband she obviously didn't like and a father-in-law she ignored when she wasn't yelling at him. The only thing they all seemed to agree on was doting on Ah-miao, their precious boy.

I sat down to have tea with them one last time. Everyone

was gloomy and quiet, a contrast to the conflict and abuse I had witnessed the first time I was there. When I stood up to leave, Old Chen went through the curtain into his room and came back with something in his hand.

He followed me out of the door. "Dong-mei, I want you to have this."

I looked up into his watery eyes, then down at the passport-sized book in his hand. The red plastic cover was dusty and split at the corners, the gold-coloured characters on the front scuffed and almost illegible. But I managed to read the three most well known characters in the language: Chairman Mao. It was a copy of the famous "Little Red Book."

"Thank you," I murmured, confused by such a strange gift.

"I hope you will find a few minutes to read part of it," he said. "I marked the place where the story of Old Man Yu Moves the Mountain begins. Read it, then you can throw the book away. I have no use for it any more."

"All right," I said. "I will."

He held my gaze, and for a second I could see the man who used to be called Old Revolutionary Chen.

"Dong-mei," he said again, looking me up and down as if he was memorizing my appearance. "I have been a fool." Then he turned and walked back into the house.

I put the little book in my backpack. Ah-miao walked me down the path to the threshing ground, where he had parked his motorcycle. He insisted on giving me a ride into the city.

"I'm sorry my parents and grandfather weren't more friendly," he said. "It has nothing to do with you. Last night I gave them some bad news. They didn't take it very well."

I waited for him to go on. Around us, the cicadas kept up their loud, monotonous buzz. The odour of growing rice rose from the paddies, and the sun beat down like a hammer. Thinking of my encounter with Ms. Song in Shanghai, I half expected Ah-miao to ask for my help in going to Canada. Maybe his parents and grandfather didn't like the idea.

"You see," he began, "I plan to get married in a few months, during the Spring Festival."

"Aren't you a little young?" I asked tactlessly, remembering the rules set by the government. "You're only eighteen!"

Ah-miao let out a laugh, revealing the gap where he had lost a tooth. "You foreigners read too much, Dong-mei. No one cares any more so long as you don't ask the government for anything, like a piece of land to put up a house."

"Oh. Then I guess your fiancée and you will move in with your parents and grandfather."

"No. There is no room for us, not while my grandfather is still alive. But even if there was, Lian-hua and I have decided to set up our new household with *her* parents."

"That *would* be bad news," I said.

"You see, Lian-hua is their only child and . . ."

"And so are you. I thought the son always brings his wife to *his* family." What I didn't say was: Isn't that what all the madness is about, wanting to have a son?

"Not any more, Half-sister. China is progressing. Forget about the old customs and traditions. Nowadays, it's money that sets the rules, does the talking, and makes the decisions. Lian-hua's family is richer than mine, way richer, and has potential to grow richer still. Her old man holds a high position in the commune, but that's not where his money really comes from. Months ago, he bought two used turtle carts and began a local taxi service. The government encourages private enterprise, you know."

"But you said he's a Party official."

"That works even better. Less red tape, more green lights to get things going. You get my point? Her father promised me that after we are married—in his house, of course, not mine—he is going to purchase a third cart and hire me as the driver, and eventually make me a partner. It means that I won't have to work in the fields any more, but most of all, some day I will be making tons of money. My old man tried to start his own business many years ago, raising rabbits or something. He lost everything. He has no fire in his belly. In many ways, he seems older and weaker than Grandfather. I should have taken you to Lian-hua's house in the Bao Family Village. It's much bigger and fancier than mine, with balconies, wood floors, ceiling lights, and wall units, all first class. Even you would be impressed."

I let him talk. I couldn't help but feel awkward hearing him brag about someone else's wealth and the advantage that marriage to Lian-hua would bring. It was so practical, not to mention in bad taste. Back home, where marriage was concerned, everything was love and passion. But here, it was power and opportunity.

That explained the sombre mood after I had arrived at Ah-miao's house. It wasn't bad news for the Chen family; it was a catastrophe. Ah-miao's plan wasn't just reversing centuries of tradition. I tried to keep a smile off my face, conscious of the irony. The boy child the Chens had done so much to get was going to leave them and join his in-laws in another village. I recalled an old Chinese expression I had learned in Frank's class, something about fetching water in a bamboo basket.

"They wanted me to find another girl," Ah-miao went on, not noticing my smile. "But they forget, it's hard to find a wife, a suitable one especially. Young men outnumber women by a big margin. On the cross-talk show, a radio comedy, they make jokes about China having the world's biggest crop of frustrated bachelors. In the old days, men who were rich and powerful had more than one wife. I guess in order to solve the problem in the future a woman will have to take in a few husbands! The whole thing is crazy, isn't it?"

No wonder, I thought, in a place where some fetuses are aborted as soon as the mother finds out by ultrasound that they're female. Or baby girls are taken care of in one way or another after they're born.

On the plane, over the Pacific Ocean, I opened the "Little Red Book" to the page Old Chen had marked for me. "Old Man Yu Moves the Mountain" was part of a speech made by Mao Ze-dong at the Seventh Central Committee Meeting of the Party, whatever that was, on June 11, 1945. Mao referred to a fable that told of an old farmer who lived in north China. Two high mountains stood in front of his house, between him and his fields. One was called Mount Tai, the other Mount Wang-wo, and the old man decided to move them with a shovel and a wheelbarrow. The fable's moral was that determination and faith and time would enable a person to conquer obstacles that appeared to be insurmountable.

Mao was still a hero to some people in China. I had seen

his portrait hanging in a couple of houses in Poplar Tree Village. Now, Ah-miao had told me, Deng Xiao-ping was the hero. But on the plane, with the red book in my hands, I remembered a TV show I had seen, some history documentary that my dad insisted I watch with him. It was about the war in Vietnam. There was a lot of footage on the last hours in Saigon, when the Americans were withdrawing and evacuating their embassy. Helicopters swept in one after another while the Viet Cong assaulted the walls. It was much more terrifying than any war movie, because it was real.

In one shot, a Vietnamese woman ran towards an already heavily laden helicopter that hovered several feet off the ground, ready to rise out of the machine-gun fire into the smoke-filled sky. In her arms was a baby. Just as the plane began to lift off, she reached the open doorway and thrust the baby into the arms of an American man inside. The helicopter shot up like an elevator car and the woman fell to the ground in a sea of smoke and fire. The terror in her eyes couldn't be described as she stood up in the swirling dust, arms at her sides, face turned to the sky as her baby disappeared from view. There was no word on what had happened to either of them.

My dad had tears in his eyes when the program was over. And I had tears in mine when I dropped the little red book into the trash bag when the flight attendant came around. Old Man Yu, Mao, and the others who made the revolution were abstractions to me. I have met one hero in my life. Her name is Chun-mei, and she is my mother.

ACKNOWLEDGEMENTS

We would like to thank Meg Taylor for her contribution to this project, Shaun Oakey for the copy edit, and John Pearce, as always, for his support and guidance. Thanks also to the Canada Council and the Ontario Arts Council.